SINNER HUNTED

Sinner Security Series

RAVEN GALE

For information contact :

sglawrenceauthor@gmail.com

https://www.slawrencewriter.com/ sign up for my newsletter to stay up to date on new releases and for exclusive giveaways

Cover design by Dissident Designs

ISBN978-1-950851-10-2

First Edition: 2021

❀ Created with Vellum

I dedicate this series to my fellow veterans. To those that face their demons daily, who see faces of the dead when they close their eyes, and hear the screams of the dying in the quiet moments.
You are not alone.

CHAPTER ONE

I'VE DONE TRULY TERRIBLE THINGS, BOT THINKS. HE HAS HAD the thought hundreds, no, thousands of times since the war.

People had died, either because of him or by his hand. The others have tried their hardest to protect him from it, the killing, but he'd signed up for it. Hadn't he?

He doesn't sleep. Not much anyway. Even now, he should be sleeping. Glancing at the clock, he sees it's later than he thought, or earlier, depending on how you look at it.

Three a.m. He rubs his eyes, his vision blurry from staring at his computer screen for hours on end, writing code and hiding their tracks as they try to locate the head of the human trafficking ring. Some days, he wishes he'd never agreed to help Ember but the way Carter is now, well, he'd do anything to help her if it keeps Carter happy and level.

Keep his demons at bay, the shadows from his eyes. Shadows that they all have. Bot thinks he's lucky. He has less than the others, but they are there lurking, waiting to break him, just like they haunt his friends.

Some days are worse than others, and today is one of those days. He glances at the chat room he has open on half his screen before typing furiously, entering the code for the other program that is displayed on the other half. He almost has him. He doesn't focus on the video that is playing, forcing himself to ignore the woman. No, not woman, girl.

He knows he's going to have more shadows from this shit. Ember now carries a few but she hides them well. Erik, their European contact, maybe Interpol, maybe MI-6, who knows, has them as well.

Erik's are harder to hide since it's him that usually goes in after Bot finds the locations. They work hard to keep the worst of it from Ember.

Joe has helped with that. He was against it until he saw one of the videos of a maybe twenty-year-old girl being sold. Live.

They didn't save her. Bot is still looking.

Refocusing on the job at hand, he keeps typing, tracking the motherfucker that is live streaming the current video.

"Gotcha, fucker."

Finally, the IP address pops up. He sends it to Erik and his team. They have been waiting for the message. Bot had narrowed it down yesterday, and they moved into the city to wait.

Placing the earbud in, he turns on the comms, running it through his computers and listening to them as they move into position.

It's what he does...listen. Carter thinks he needs to protect him. Bot shakes his head at the thought. *I'm not a fucking kid; haven't been since Afghanistan.*

The saying is war is hell, but the real hell comes after, when you have to learn to live with what you had to do. He pushes away the memories that are threatening to break loose from the box he keeps them locked in. Instead, he focuses on the girl in the video.

She might be mid-twenties. They have her made up in

thick make-up and trashy lingerie. Why, he doesn't know. The really sick perverts like them more virginal. Maybe this is a special auction.

She is trying to do what they want, but her eyes are filled with terror. It's killing him. His fist hits the table. Suddenly, the feed goes black. Comms are silent. Then all hell breaks loose. Bot holds his breath.

"Clear," Erik murmurs. "We got her, Bot." He lets the breath out in a puff.

One more saved. Hundreds, thousands, hell, maybe a million more to go.

He sends a message to Ember even as he listens to the sounds of the girl crying through Erik's link. She keeps saying 'thank you' over and over.

"We'll get her to a safe place, Bot. Let Ember and the others know, please."

"Will do, Erik," he responds, his voice flat, his emotions locked down tight.

"And Bot, good job. You know we couldn't do any of this without your skills."

Had Erik heard the self-loathing in his voice?

"Thanks." Bot turns off the comms, not wanting to hear anymore.

He should sleep. Pushing away from his screens, he stands and stretches. His spine cracks and pops from too many hours in the chair. Sweeping all the empty cans and wrappers into the trash can, he climbs the stairs and punches the keypad at the top, waiting as the steel door slides open.

The sun blinds him as it comes in the windows over the kitchen sink, forcing him to stand there to let his eyes adjust before moving around the island to the refrigerator. Opening it, he sees pretty much nothing, having forgotten to shop again. He turns to the pantry and opens that door. Protein shake it is, then. Mixing it as he stands at the sink, he stares out at the mountains.

The whole team lives in Colorado, at least part-time. Joe still has his house out in the swamp somewhere. Bot bought this place in Breckenridge to stay close to the office. They travel a lot, and while he can work from anywhere, he likes to run operations either from where they are taking place, if they will let him, or from the office.

He runs Ember's project from the locked basement here. He keeps it out of sight.

Hidden.

Lots of things are hidden in that room.

CHAPTER TWO

HE'S GETTING CARELESS, JOE THINKS IN BOTH SADNESS AND anger. Joe watches Bot through the scope, shaking his head as Bot stands there lost in thought in front of a huge fucking window.

Joe pulls out his phone, keeping an eye to the scope even while pressing Carter's number.

"Hey. We need to talk about the kid." He doesn't wait for Carter to even say hello.

"Good morning, Joe."

"Yeah, yeah, good morning. He's getting worse, Carter."

Joe's best friend sighs, and he can picture him rubbing his hand over his face.

"I've watched for the last twenty-four hours, and he's not slept or eaten. Right at this very moment, he is staring into space in front of his big window, not paying one bit attention. He can't feel my eyes on him, Carter."

"He's getting worse." Umm, that's what Joe's been fucking saying for months, so he doesn't bother doing it again.

"He's lost weight and looks like shit." He squints down the scope one last time before pushing up.

Holding the phone between his shoulder and ear, he packs the scope and his pad away into the bag. He listens to Carter as he talks over options of what they can do.

"It's time, Carter," Joe says, though they've both been avoiding it for three years.

"Are you sure?" Joe can hear the worry that the entire team feels about their youngest member.

"I think so." He rubs a hand over his head.

"I'll be there in forty. Wait for me, Joe."

Joe rolls his eyes. "Yes, Dad." He smiles as Carter grumbles. "Bring Ember. He won't argue with her."

"Like I had a choice." Joe can hear her yelling about being ready in five minutes and how he better not leave her behind.

"See ya in a few." Joe hangs up and sits back, leaning against the tree to wait.

It only takes him moments to fall asleep. Years of grabbing naps every time the bullets or bombs stopped trained his brain to quiet quickly.

He hears the rumble of Carter's SUV long before it comes into sight and straightens, bowing backwards to stretch his back. He's on his feet and loping across the uneven ground in seconds. He makes it to the side of Carter's vehicle just as he shuts off the engine.

The door doesn't open immediately, and Joe can hear him talking quietly to Ember. No warning is going to prepare her for this fight. Not many people know or have seen the side of Bot that they are about to encounter. Not only is it the mean side, but underneath that vicious anger will be the hurt. That's what no one ever sees.

He's going to be fucking pissed they brought her into this, but she is Joe's secret weapon, her and the tears he knows will start falling when she gets sight of Bot. Joe walks around to her side and earns a grin when he pulls open her door and holds out his hand.

"Joe." It sounds sweet as honey on her tongue.

"Cher." He leans in and kisses her cheek. "In another life, I'd take you away from all this."

"Really?" Her eyebrow raises slightly and she glances back at the love of her life and his best friend, who is giving them both a fake frown. "Well, if he keeps up his craziness, it won't take another life."

Joe grins as he helps her down. This girl loves to poke the bear. As soon as her feet hit the ground, she is stomping away and right up the front steps. Her fist comes up, and she pounds on the heavy steel door that looks like wood. It sounds like S.W.A.T. is about to break through. Damn, she really is worried.

"You open this door, Colin Matthew Martin, open it right this minute."

Shit, she's making Joe's Grand-mere proud, using the middle name and all.

"Jesus fucking Christ, woman, I'm coming." Bot's voice is filled with irritation and exhaustion when it booms through the security speaker by the door. "What the fuck are you all doing here?"

"Quit cussing at her." Carter's tone is low and deadly and it draws a glare from the 'her' in question.

"Just open the door." Joe is tired of his shit. Hell, he's just tired. Time to get this over with.

The sound of locks, both electric and simple deadbolts, echo through the trees surrounding them. Finally, Bot throws the door open, and icy blue eyes, the whites mostly red, stare at the three of them. Ember makes a noise, and Joe knows he was right in calling them in because Bot instantly softens.

"Why didn't you say anything?" She is practically in tears already.

"I'm fine, just tired."

"Bullshit." Joe glares at him as he pushes past, strolling into Bot's house.

The other two follow as Bot stands holding the door with a pained look on his face. The place is a fucking disaster, and Ember wrinkles her nose at the smell.

"Jesus, Colin, it smells like shit in here." She ain't sugar-coating nothing for him today. "I just don't understand."

She looks at Carter and then at Joe, waiting for them to explain everything. How can they, though? How do you explain that the darkness is taking over, that he's losing his battle with everything that haunts him, that haunts them?

"Colin, please talk to me." She walks over and takes one of his hands in hers. "Please help me."

Joe watches him close, and so does Carter. They can both see him tensing, see the anger building. Uncontrollable rage. He jerks his hand free.

"Get out!" He screams right in her face.

"No." She says it quietly but refuses to back down. "I did this. Oh my god, why didn't you tell me? I would've found another way. Erik would have helped me or suggested someone to help."

Now the tears are flowing. His face fills with guilt and pain, but he refuses to let go of the anger.

"I said leave, Ember." He looks over her at the others. "Take her and go."

"You know better than that, Bot. We ain't leaving." Joe shrugs. "It's been too long. You've fallen too far down the hole. I've been watching you for a few days. You don't eat or sleep. Hell, this place looks like a shit, and so do you."

Carter steps forward, drawing Bot's gaze. "We've decided it's time for you to take some time off and go home. Your mom is expecting you."

"Are you fucking kidding me? You called my mom?" He paces away then turns back. "I'm not going."

He walks away down the hall. They look at each other, and Ember stands and starts toward the kitchen. Joe follows her while Carter gets on the phone, making plans for an unwilling passenger. No commercial flight will do. This is going to be A-team style all the way.

Ember opens the pantry and pulls out trash bags and other cleaning supplies. She doesn't speak as she gets started.

She won't be leaving until he gives in.

Joe is willing to knock his ass out, if it means saving him from himself.

CHAPTER THREE

THEY HAVE INVADED MY HOME.

Bot's thought is not entirely incorrect but it is the anger talking. The rage won't go away, and neither will they. He punches the wall, adding another hole.

He doesn't want to take it out on them but he knows they won't hate him forever. He lets his eyes close but jerks them open within seconds. He can't stand the faces that are burned on the inside of the lids.

It's why he doesn't sleep. He sees them all but mostly he sees James. His best friend, the one he followed into the Army. He sees him die every time his eyes close. So he doesn't sleep. Now many others join James...soldiers, women, and children. He imagines every woman and child they don't save, but James is with each of them.

His phone vibrates, and he looks down at it on his dresser, his mom's face appearing. He ignores it, like he has for the last six months. She will leave a message, like she does every day. Every day for the last year. Since she visited and realized he wasn't ever coming back home.

Ever.

He can't face them. None of them.

They can't and don't understand.

Bottles clank together from the other room, and his molars grind together. Fuck. Opening the door, he looks down the hall and sees Ember raking things off the coffee table into a trash bag. She still has tears running down her face.

"Please. Just go." He doesn't say it loudly, but Carter steps out into the hall, his eyes locked on Bot. Joe is right behind him.

Ember doesn't even look up. She knows they are about to start the argument again. No point in her getting yelled at by Bot again, even if it sounds great in his British accent. Asshole. Joe drops the bag of trash that he is holding onto the floor by more trash. Carter is striding right for Bot, but he starts to close the door. Carter's eyes narrow and behind him, Joe shakes his head.

"You're pushing our limits, Bot." Joe's Cajun accent is thick with anger. "We're trying to help you, son."

"I'm not your son. I don't need your help." Bot pauses, giving them a hard look.

They return it with a couple that might be harder.

"You close that door, and I'm going to rip it off the hinges." Carter's voice is quiet and deadly. Bot recognizes it from the war. Carter is serious. If he can't do it with his body, he will blow it off.

"I'm not going home."

Both Carter and Joe see the instant Bot quits fighting. Bot knows that they aren't going to give up and he doesn't want his house destroyed by the battle that would come if he kept fighting them.

"Why don't we take a walk?" Carter leaves no room for argument, and they start to follow him out.

Bot stops when he gets near Ember. "Don't clean. You

don't need to." His hand touches her forearm, trying to stop it as she scrubs at the table.

"Someone does." She looks up and lets him see her face streaked with tears. "Someone needs to clean up all of this."

She doesn't just mean the trash and moldy dishes, and he knows it. He doesn't say anything else. How can he argue with her assessment of him and his home? He follows the others out, face lowered slightly, feeling like shit for upsetting them all.

They don't speak to him until they are out of Ember's earshot, not wanting to upset her even more. Bot waits, fighting the urge to run, disappear into the trees. His eyes dart around the area, checking the trees and any shadows. Joe might think he hasn't been looking, paying attention, but he has cameras hidden everywhere and screens filled with images. He watches. He sees too much maybe. It's true he didn't see Joe, but he knew someone was out there, watching him. He just didn't care, resigning himself to the bullet that will eventually come.

The one that he thinks he deserves. He had started trying to make it easier for the ghosts to get him because he's not strong enough to do it himself.

He looks back at those he considers friends, brothers even, and they are watching him close. Here it comes.

"I've rented a jet. You will get on it and you will go home." Bot grinds his molars at Carter's tone, or rather, Captain Sterling's tone, because it's not his friend standing in front of him. It's the commander of the unit. The man in question sighs. "It's time, Bot. James isn't..."

Bot doesn't hear the rest as he spins away and stalks into the trees. He doesn't want to hear the same old shit again. How would they know what James would fucking want? James wanted to be alive but he's not.

"That's not your fault, Bot." Joe is right behind him.

"Get the fuck out of here, Magic."

"No." Grabbing the younger man, Joe spins him around, throwing up his arms to block the fist swing toward his face. "You don't want to go there with me." Bot swings again, and Joe moves into him.

Bot is so lost in the darkness, in the past, that he didn't see it coming and hits the ground hard. Joe stands over him looking down. There is no anger on his face or in his eyes but understanding, and maybe that's what finally breaks through.

"You aren't the only one that lost someone, Bot. You aren't the only one that wishes they could go back and trade places, but we can't. You can't. So it's time to move forward. Or die." He steps back, keeping his eyes on the young man, on the storms rolling through his blue eyes. "Your choice. We are here, your brothers and sister, and we'll help you though if you let us. If you don't, then you leave us to mourn one more fallen. Shitty fucking thing to do to us, but it's your decision. I will expect you to explain to Ember. She doesn't deserve to live with the guilt."

Bot pushes up while shaking his head.

"Make no mistake, she will blame herself." Joe spins away and leaves the man to make his decision.

Bot watches his retreating back and then looks beyond to his house. Carter is standing with his arms around his wife, and she is shaking her head at whatever he is saying. Her face swings around as Joe steps from the tree line. Ember tries to break free, but Carter shakes his head and holds her until Joe reaches them.

Bot remains where he is, watching as they try to talk to her. Tries to explain. How do you explain that he's tired of hiding and tired of the guilt? She doesn't want to hear or understand because she, at least subconsciously, knows it could happen to any of them. Bot sees the look of desperation, and she looks between the two of them. He recognizes the moment she realizes it could be either of them.

Ember cares for them all, but Carter and Joe have her heart. Standing, he starts towards them, stopping at the tree line. They can't hold her then. She is flying across the yard at him in less than a second. They both stay where they are and watch as she crashes into him, clinging to him like she believes she has the power to banish the ghosts.

If only it was that easy.

"Please." She says it low as she hugs him tight. "I can't imagine and I won't say that I can, but please try a little bit more for me. For them." Bot feels her swallow hard before she continues. "I don't want to lose you and I'm afraid if they lost you, I'd lose them too. I wouldn't survive that. You hold our fates in your hands, Colin." She leans back and looks at him hard. "No pressure." She smiles slightly.

"I can't promise you anything, Ember, but please believe me when I say this has nothing to do with anything you asked me to do." Her chin begins to quake, and he closes his eyes for a moment. He misses her quick grin and the shaking of the other men's heads. She has won. "Okay, I'll go but I'm just going to see my mom real quick. Then I'm leaving."

He only hopes he can avoid James' family.

The other men watch as Bot lets Ember lead him to the back deck. They continue to watch him closely as he grabs some things and shoves them in a bag. In fact, he has one of the three at his side the entire morning. Even as he climbs the steps to the small private plane, the three of them follow right behind him.

Ducking as he goes in, he shakes his head when he straightens and turns to the right. The team, minus Jacques, is sitting in seats scattered around the plane. They say nothing, just nod as he makes his way by them to the seat farthest in the back. Carter and Ember sit in the middle seats that seem to have been saved for them. Joe flops down opposite Bot and stretches out his legs.

"Total A-Team trip," he murmurs as he pulls a worn and frayed ball cap down over his eyes.

He is asleep before take off, and when they are finally cruising at forty-thousand feet, Ember stops at their seats on her way back to the restroom or the bedroom.

She smiles at Joe sprawling and snoring softly. Leaning down, her lips brush against Bot's ear. "He was watching you for a few days." She says nothing else before she straightens and continues back.

Days. Damn fool hadn't slept, Bot is sure of it.

CHAPTER FOUR

CARTER WATCHES AS BOT FINALLY DRIFTS OFF TO SLEEP. JOE had basically trapped him in his seat, unless he wanted to climb over the back. The tall Cajun was slick, he'd give him that. He had forced the younger man to rest. Viper is watching them both close.

They all know Bot isn't the only one that doesn't sleep much, but Joe is going to be much harder to crack. The nightmares will come, but they all hope the two men get some rest.

One crisis at a time.

Carter's eyes move around the plane, slowly taking them all in before movement from the back draws them. A smile curves his lips, and for just a moment, he forgets the others. Ember is standing at the opening of the hallway and she is looking at Joe with soft, love-filled eyes. Another man might be jealous, but not Carter; he knows he owns her heart and he loves that she loves his unit, or as she calls them, her tribe. She looks up and grins at him, and he can do nothing other than return it.

He tears his gaze from her and then notices Celt shaking

his head. "Yer a lovesick fool." Carter shakes his head in agreement. "'Tis good to see."

Ember sits, and Celt winks at her before turning back to the hand-held game system in his hand. His fingers move at the speed of light as he plays his game, grumbling under his breath.

Ember threads her fingers through Carter's, and he thinks, no, wishes they could all have exactly what he has. Her head lays on his shoulder, and he rests his against her, letting his eyes drift closed as she gives his hand a gentle squeeze.

Her eyes are drifting like his did moments ago. She sees so much more than they think she does. She worries more than they know. But she has a plan. A sly smile curves her lips as she thinks about it. When she refocuses, pushing the idea running through her head away, she sees Adder watching her, his head moving slowly from side to side.

She gives him an innocent look, which he doesn't buy for one second. He shakes his head again before leaning his head back against the seat and closing his eyes. Everyone uses the long flight time to get some uninterrupted rest, everyone except Carter, who keeps a close eye on Bot. He sees the minute the dreams start.

He shifts Ember slightly, and she wakes immediately. He nods at the younger man. She looks towards the back of the plane and sees the frown creasing Bot's face, watches him jerk in his sleep. Carter stands and makes his way quietly back to Joe, who has straightened.

He squats beside his best friend, and they talk quietly as the others begin to shift in their seats. No one touches Bot as he starts to fight his demons; they all just watch with shadows of their own demons in their eyes.

Ember watches with her heart breaking.

It doesn't take long before he comes awake with a shout

that causes them all to flinch. His eyes are wild until they focus on Joe and Carter. Instantly they fill with shame, but both men shake their head.

"We are almost there, kid." They don't say anything about the nightmare.

The others pretend to be engrossed with other things, protecting one of their own. He takes several deep breaths before he starts to relax. He turns his face to the window and stares out, not saying a word for the rest of the flight.

The tension is stretched tight as a drum when the pilot finally announces their descent.

There is a car waiting when the plane lands, and the team circles Bot as if he is a client. But in reality, they are all just on alert for him to run. They all know that Colin hasn't been home since they all separated and started the security firm. He's on his home turf and could do a runner and disappear.

Bot wants to roll his eyes at their insanity but refrains as Ember links her arm with his. She looks up, and he nods at her. A silent promise. A promise to see this through as best as he can. It won't include seeing James' family.

The door opens on the car, and he sees his mom sitting in the back seat. Ever the stoic British woman that she is, there are no tears as her head turns in his direction. She scoots across the seat and climbs out. She doesn't speak to him but instead goes directly up to Carter and hugs him tightly. Their voices are low, and Bot doesn't try to hear. Why bother he knows it's about him?

He does hear her say 'thank you,' and it makes him feel like shit. He knows he's a shit son, but her gratitude for them dragging him here just highlights how much of one he is. Joe's hand comes down hard on his shoulder and squeezes it for a minute before releasing then pushing him forward gently.

"It's time, Bot." Joe looks down at his friend, the little brother he never had. "We will be around. If you need us."

Bot can only nod his head. How does one act when one is heading out to face demons that could destroy them? He doesn't know.

"Go rest. You've earned it, Colin. You deserve it." Ember leans her head against his shoulder and squeezes his forearm before stepping away to Carter. His mom holds out her hand, and he takes it. She smiles up at him and memories of holding her hand when he was little play through his mind.

CHAPTER FIVE

IT'S BEEN WEEKS. COLIN STARES OUT THE WINDOW, watching as people move down the street. His mother watches from the crack of the open door, worry clouding her eyes that match her son's. He has barely left the room and is silent most of the time. Except at night. At night, he cries out for his friend, for help, and then he paces until morning.

Each morning, she forces him to eat, and then he returns to the chair and stares out at the street. She turns away quietly, then heads to her bedroom, closing the door. Sitting on the bed, she cries silently into her hands. She has no idea how to help her boy.

He's only getting worse. A door slams, and she jerks, her head turning to her own door. Colin is the only one in the house. His footsteps pause outside her door before continuing down the stairs. She waits a moment then rises, crossing to her bathroom. Cold water splashing over her face washes away the tears and hides some of the redness.

Taking a deep breath, she straightens her spine and leaves her room, going down the stairs to find her baby. He has been the most important thing in her life since the day he was born. She stops on the bottom step, looking at the picture of James and Colin. It seems to be from another life. She supposes it could be, depending on how you think of it. There is the 'before James died' and the 'after James died.'

She's read everything on survivor's guilt, but it hasn't helped her help him. She finds him standing at the garden door, staring out of it.

"Colin?"

He turns, and she sees rage and a soul-deep sadness on his face.

"What's wrong?" She knows but she hopes today he will be able to answer.

He shakes his head, his teeth grinding together. "I saw them."

She sighs, but this time, it's in relief. "Candace and Margot?" She knew but again hoped he'd be able to talk about it a little.

He nods and turns back to the window. She hesitates but can't stop herself from going to him. She wraps her arms around him, laying her cheek against his shoulder. He stiffens for a second but then he relaxes against her a little.

"Did you tell them?" He whispers the question.

"No, baby, I didn't." She hugs him tighter for a second as he relaxes even more. "You asked me not to and I haven't, but..."

Bot shakes his head. "I can't, mom."

"They really want to talk to you. They want to hear what happened from you." She holds him tight as he tries to get away from her and away from her words. "They need to hear the details from someone who loved him as much as they do. Someone who misses him as much."

He stares out, unable to respond to her. Tears burn at his eyes. Tears that he's kept at bay for years.

"They made a memorial for him; you should visit." He

shakes his head at her suggestion. The very thought of going and sitting at some depressing headstone with his name engraved on it makes him so angry and so guilty he can't even see straight.

She lets him go as he pulls away. He stalks out the door into the garden and starts to pace. She doesn't go to him, doesn't try to stop him as he throws over her chairs. He will fix it all when he's done, just like he has numerous times since he arrived.

Her phone vibrates, and she reaches back, pulling it from her pocket to look at the screen. It's Joe, checking in like he has every day. She answers, pulling the doors closed so Colin can't hear her.

"He's out in the garden."

"Tearing up your furniture again?" He chuckles, but she can hear the worry under the humor.

"A little, but he always fixes it. I'm not sure this is going to work. I think... I might be making it worse," she admits while wiping away the tears that have pooled at the edge of her lashes.

"No, you aren't, ma'am. He just doesn't have work to bury himself in, so it's all there staring him in the face."

She kind of hates his softer tone, wishing for the joking Joe, not the sincere one.

Colin turns and looks at her, regret stamped on his face.

"I need to go; he's calming down."

She doesn't need to say anymore. Joe knows what comes next. He's felt everything the kid is feeling and took it all out on his family and friends. Still does, sometimes.

They hang up with quick goodbyes, and she opens the door to the garden as she slides the phone back in her pocket.

"I'm so sorry, Mom." He starts to crumple, and once again, she rushes to wipe away her baby's tears, all while murmuring softly to him.

He lets her hold him for a long time before finally pulling away and moving to right the chairs he threw across her small garden. He doesn't say anything when he passes her to go back inside, but his hand reaches out and grabs hers, squeezing it for just a second before he retreats back to his room.

It's not much, but she will take it.

CHAPTER SIX

BOT SHAKES HIS HEAD EVEN AS HE HOLDS IT IN HIS HANDS. The sun has set and he's been leaning against the wall for hours, since he left his mom in the garden. He hates seeing the look of pity on her face.

"I should leave." His words are whispered and filled with self-loathing.

Pushing up, he grabs his bag from the closet at his left and throws it on the bed. He stands, listening to his mom moving around in her bedroom. He hates that this is going to break her heart.

How can he stay though? "I'll end up hurting her."

His phone vibrates, and he looks down. He's been ignoring everyone's calls, but this is a number from close to home. Erik.

"Hey. Where have you been, Bot?" Erik's voice is hard. "I've been trying to reach you. I asked your entire team, but they had nothing to say."

"I'm visiting my mom." He doesn't elaborate.

"So you're close. Good. I could use your help. We are getting ready to go pull some girls out. We found an auction right here in London."

Bot closes his eyes and takes a deep breath. More women and kids being forced to do unspeakable things.

"Send me the address. I'll leave in five." He pushes the end button then turns and grabs some things, throwing them into the bag. The text comes through in seconds.

He is silent as he moves down the hallway, stopping in the kitchen to write a quick note to his mom. An apology for once again breaking her heart.

Then he slips out the door and into the night. He's down the street in less than a minute and to the train station in five, just fast enough to catch the last train into the city. He sits alone after turning off his phone, his back against the wall, eyes darting around the car.

There are only a few stops between his town and London a few people get on. Mostly drunks looking to get home, and all of them give him a wide berth.

Erik is waiting as he climbs the stairs at the station. He nods and then follows the man to a car.

"The team is already in place. We're down a man because of an injury." Erik glances at Bot in the passenger seat. "Are you good?"

"Five by five," Bot responds instantly with the military slang, knowing Erik won't believe he's perfect or even near it.

He looks at the man driving, daring him to say otherwise.

"Why wouldn't anyone tell me where you were?" Erik's eyes narrow slightly.

"I told them I didn't want to be found. I needed a break." He watches, making sure Erik believes him.

The man slowly nods before turning his face back to the road. "Well, I'm glad you answered." He glances at his watch. "The auction is set to start in thirty minutes. We have just enough time to get there and get you geared up."

"Do you have a van for me?" Bot asks, not expecting the answer he gets.

"No, man, we need you to go in with us."

Sweat beads over Bot's body as he tenses at the idea of going in, of being responsible for another person. "Okay."

His voice doesn't sound convincing at all.

"I need you to get the girls, Bot." Erik glances his way once again.

"Okay. I can do that."

"If anything goes wrong, ANYTHING, take them to this address." He holds out a small piece of paper. "Memorize it."

Bot reads the address, committing it to memory. "Do you think anything is going to go wrong?"

Erik seems more tense than usual, but then again, Bot usually only deals with him through his monitor and headset.

"I just don't like how they keep slipping away."

Bot reads between the lines. Erik thinks he has a mole, or a leak. Bot nods, considering all their previous operations.

"When I get back, I'll go through all the footage." He doesn't say anything else as they stop behind a large lorry.

In seconds, both men have climbed out of the car and into the back of waiting truck. They have a bag waiting for Bot, and he begins to get ready. He's done in just a few minutes, muscle memory taking over as his mind tries to solve the puzzle Erik has placed before him. His eyes drift over each team member, looking for any sign of treachery. He sees nothing. Could he have been hacked?

The feed or the connection? His head shakes in denial. No way. It must be something else. Someone else.

"Comm check." He gives Erik a thumbs up, and so do the rest of the team.

"Okay, let's go. Bot, you're with me." The others rush out into the darkness and disappear. Erik and Bot walk in the front door, both dressed in black suits. A bidder and his guard. Bot breaks away as soon as the lights dim. A man drags a young girl out under a spotlight.

She is terrified, but they can't stop the auction. The plan is to let it go until finished. Previously, the women and girls or boys are kept in a room until then. Bot's job is to find them as the last one is in the spotlight and get them out. Erik will grab the last one from the main room as the rest of the team captures or kills the men running it.

Many hours and countless bids later, Bot makes his way around the edge of the room, sticking to the shadows, getting ready to follow the handler back to the room. He slides along the wall until he reaches a doorway that he steps into as he watches the man jerk the child along before stopping almost at the end of the corridor.

He stays hidden as the man makes a return trip, this time dragging a young boy. It takes all his willpower not to kill him right as he passes by his hiding spot. Once he's alone in the silent hall, he taps the earpiece.

"I've found the room. Let me know when they announce the final item."

"Copy," Erik replies.

The minutes drag by, each one seeming like an hour, but he stays put, watching as, one by one, the captives are taken out and sold to the highest bidder.

"Last one," Erik says over the comms. "Everyone in place. On my go."

Bot watches as the man takes a crying woman back to the room and comes back out, pulling a girl that couldn't be any older than twelve. She has beautiful, long white-blonde hair and a scattering of freckles over her cheeks, which are flushed pink. Bot is impressed with her as she holds her head high and stares forward in defiance. No tears from this little hellcat. He's glad that they will get her to safety before she loses that.

"Go."

Bot races down the hall and kicks the door open, holding his hands out. "I'm here to get you away from the others. I need you to come with me."

They all cower except one woman. She stands in front of the rest, ready to defend them if it's needed. Footsteps pound down the hall. "We need to go! Now!"

She nods, turning to speak quickly to the others, and they all run at him. He holds a hand up to stop them as he turns drawing his gun. The man he'd wanted to kill all night slides to a stop in front of the open door. Bot raises the gun, firing in one smooth motion. The bastard falls dead, and Bot kicks him out of the way, ignoring the crying happening behind him.

"Let's go." He starts slowly down the hall.

"More are coming in. Bot, take them like we planned." Erik sounds calm, but Bot can hear the anger underneath.

He was right. He has a leak.

"Follow me." Bot turns right instead of left and races down the hall. He had glanced at the layout of the building and knows there should be a stairwell at the end. When he stops, he turns to watch as they catch up. "We need to move fast and quiet. Older ones carry the smallest." He reaches for a young girl with a head of wild curls. She is sucking her thumb, and his heart breaks for the damage already done to her.

They run. They run down the stairs and then through the streets.

Bot kills two more times before he thinks they are safe to head to the safe house.

It is dawn when he finally knocks softly on the door of a posh house. Luckily, it has a high fence with ivy growing on it surrounding the front. His charges hide in the shadows as Bot waits to find out if this will really be a safe haven for them.

The door cracks open, and her hair looks like it on fire in the morning light. Amazing hazel eyes with multiple shades of green and blue mixed with a little gold stare out at him.

"Bot?" He wonders how she knows. "Erik showed me your picture." Those amazing eyes glance around her garden. "How many?"

"Ten."

"So many." She is angry and sad at the high number. "Bring them in."

He doesn't move though, not one to trust easily, and he doesn't know this woman.

"Would you like to check the house? It's just me here. It was my family's home here in the city, but it's just me now."

He hates how defeated she looks after her admission. He makes a decision and turns his head, nodding once. They all break from their hiding places. The little girl he had carried runs for him, wrapping her arms around his legs and burying her face.

The woman in the doorway makes a sound of distress. "He told me, but I had no idea. Not really."

She shakes her head, eyebrows drawing down as she watches the rest draw near. Suddenly, he sees her shake it off, and a smile brightens her face.

"Come in, come in. You'll be safe here for as long as you need," she promises, bending down to make eye contact with the younger ones, nodding to the teenagers and the adult woman.

They all follow her in, with Bot going last. He turns and looks out at the street, eyes quartering the area looking for anyone who could have followed them here. When he is satisfied, he closes the door and turns the lock. She is standing just behind him and reaches to the wall and sets the alarm.

He turns facing her. She smiles softly and holds out her hand. "I'm Ruby."

"Bot. Colin." He holds her hand a moment longer than he needs but he can't seem to let it go.

"Why don't I get them settled? I have rooms ready. Just in case."

CHAPTER SEVEN

Bot watches her as she leads the group through the house. Most don't want a room to themselves so they divide into groups. The youngest will stay with the woman. The teenagers pile into a room together. In the end, only the girl clinging to his leg is left.

Ruby leads him to one last room. He looks down at the little girl then reaches down and lifts her up. He holds her up so he can look at her face.

"Can you tell me your name?" She shakes her head, her thumb still in her mouth. "Do you want to stay with me or go with the others?" Her arm tightens on him. "Me, it is."

He smiles slightly at the woman as she smiles back at him.

"I'll leave you two to get settled." She turns and then stops looking back at him. "I'll be downstairs if you need anything."

She intrigues him, but the tiny girl clinging to him is his first priority. The girl is depending on him. Stepping into the room, he leaves the door open slightly, giving her the ability to run to the others if she decides that staying with a man she doesn't know is not the way to go. He sits her on the bed, gently pulling her hands free before straightening.

He pulls a chair from the corner to the side of the bed, and she starts to relax. He hopes she can fall asleep. She does in minutes, and while it might be a restless one, it's sleep all the same. He dozes, but his own dreams keep him from any actual rest. His phone vibrates, and he rubs at his eyes as he pulls his phone out of his pocket. A message from Erik.

Bot responds, letting him know they made it to the safe house. His phone vibrates again, an incoming call.

"I've called in some favors. Transport will be there to get the women and children by midmorning. I'm not using my team."

Bot hates to say but he knows it's the right call.

"Who should I be looking for?"

Erik chuckles. "Your team."

Fuck. That's not what Bot wanted to hear. Magic is going to be very angry, and Ember is going to be hurt. They are going to require an explanation.

"You want to tell me why Mercury sounded so angry?"

Bot shakes his head, not really. "No." He stands, moving away from the bed and stopping when he reaches the doorway. "It's none of your business and it isn't Carter's either."

"Have it your way." Bot imagines Erik shrugging. "Can I count on your help to find the traitor?"

"Of course." The man didn't even need to ask. Bot wants blood for the women and children they have lost because of that bastard.

"I'll contact you in a couple of days." He disconnects before Bot can respond.

He steps out into the hall, leaving the door open so she can see him across the hall if she wakes. He slides down the wall, as exhaustion hits him like a ton of bricks. He lowers his head, his emotions threatening to overwhelm him.

Ruby makes no noise as she walks, her brother had taught her how, but as she tops the stairs, she watches as he raises his head, slightly turning his face to look at her. She stares into his eyes, seeing the same ghosts that haunted Mark's.

She swallows away the tears that threaten to fall. Now is not the time. Colin doesn't look away, just watches as she draws near. She stops in front of him before moving to his side and sliding down to join him on the floor.

"You okay?" Ruby watches as he swallows hard before answering his question.

"I will be." He attempts a smile. "How do you know Erik?"

How much should she tell him? She wonders what Erik told him. "Who did he say I was?"

Mark had also taught her how not to give too much away. Interrogation techniques. He had been so excited when he had finished that training. So excited to teach her behind their parents' backs, for it wasn't something a woman of her standing would need to know. She glances at some of the paintings hanging on the wall across from them. They've been there for generations, proof of the family's standing, not that they've done anything to save it.

"Just said this was a safe place. The women and children would be safe until we can move them to Interpol custody." She can tell he knows that's not the extent of it. "Erik keeps things close to the vest."

Boy, does she know it. She also wonders about why Erik asked her to open her home.

"I've known Erik since I was a child. He was friends with my older brother." Was. She hates that word. "His parents and my parents traveled in the same social circles. He knew I had this huge house to myself, so..."

She trails off. Colin wonders why she is alone; she's beautiful and, as far as he can tell, kind. Maybe she hasn't found a suitable husband. He doesn't travel in the same social circles. His family is working class, and she is posh, upper class, probably a title somewhere in the family tree. He smiles a little, because that means so is Erik. He tucks that knowledge away.

"You didn't know that about Erik." She smiles, shaking her head at his grin. "His family is even higher than ours." She raises her eyebrows and nods at him.

"No way, that fucking asshole?" He looks at her face. "Damn, sorry."

Ruby laughs, and the sound of it ensnares him. "I have a brother that was special forces, Colin. I've heard the word 'fuck' before."

Somehow it sounds sexy as hell coming from her lips. He just blinks.

"Your brother worked with Erik?" She nods but doesn't offer more information. "You said you are alone." She nods again and once more doesn't offer more.

"Are you hungry?" He lets her change the subject. It's not hard to see that she doesn't want to talk about it.

"I could eat but I don't want to leave." He looks across at the darkened bedroom.

"Do you think you got them soon enough?"

"I think so. At least the young ones. Unfortunately, it was their innocence the bastards were buying." His rage flares to life and he clenches his fists, trying to control it.

His gaze jumps down when her hand closes over one of those fists. "You saved them, Colin. They might be changed, but you saved them from the unthinkable." He can only nod, his throat tight with emotion. "Some can't or won't be saved."

He hears the heartache in those words and he wonders who she lost and to what. Parents, brother, or lover? The last makes a flame of jealousy flare to life, and it confuses him. He doesn't know her but he can't deny the instant attraction.

His phone vibrates, and he pulls it out once again. "Erik?"

He shakes his head before answering her.

"My team. Erik called them in to help."

"Are you working with the Americans he met in Denver?" Colin blinks slow at her. How much has Erik told her? Is his team compromised? She sees something in his eyes. "He just said he met some good people that he's helping and who help him with his job."

"Sorry. I..." What can he say to explain?

"They're your family; it's natural to want to protect them." Again, something in her tone says she knows exactly what that means. "I'll go grab you some food."

She pushes up, and he sits watching her walk away. He likes the sway of her slim hips and can't help but think he's been too long without a woman. She's out of his league though, but it won't stop him from fantasizing about it.

He glances down at the phone in his hand. Two hours and they'll be here. The door down the hall opens, and the woman steps out. She looks like she's slept as much as he has.

Walking on the wood floor in her bare feet, she is quiet but not silent, not like Ruby. Her eyes are red, swollen from crying, and her accent is thick when she speaks.

"Thank you for saving them." She glances toward the closed doors then back at him.

"We saved you too." She shakes her head. Fuck. "My friends are coming to get all of you soon, to take you someplace safer so you can go home."

"I can't."

"They won't care. Your family just wants you back, I promise." She shakes her head again. "You don't have to decide now." He tries to calm her; he can tell she is ready to bolt.

Footsteps on the stairs cause the woman to spin, her body shaking in instant terror. Bot stands slowly not wanting to scare her more.

"It's just Ruby, our host." His voice is low and even. She nods but stays tense, ready to run if she needs to get away.

Ruby stops when she sees them. She holds the plate out in front of her. "I can get more if you're hungry." The woman shakes her head.

"Would you stay here and I'll go downstairs to get everything ready so we can get you to safety as soon as possible?" Bot looks across the hall at the room where the smallest victim is sleeping. "Can you watch her?"

He hopes giving her the job will calm her some. "I have protected them all."

He nods at her declaration. "I know you saved them. Now we can work together to keep them safe, get them home to their parents." She nods.

"Okay. I will watch." She moves across and stands with her back against the wall. A guard. A protector.

Bot nods then moves down the hall and takes the plate from Ruby. He turns and takes it back, holding it out to her. She takes it, careful not to touch his fingers. She was hurt badly.

"What's your name? I'm," he pauses before continuing, "Colin." Bot doesn't hide behind his call sign, like he usually does.

Something about this house or these people are getting under Bot's skin. He turns away from her, nodding his head as he does. Ruby is still standing where he left her and as he reaches her, she reaches out for him. He's once again surprised when her fingers thread through his. Part of him wants to pull away but he wants her touch more.

"I'M MARTA." He smiles slightly at the whispered reply that comes from behind him.

CHAPTER EIGHT

RUBY WATCHES AS THE CHILDREN ARE TAKEN OUT. THE woman, Ember, stands at her side; they have both grown quiet after talking for thirty minutes. Most of those minutes were used to discuss Colin. Ruby can tell Ember is very worried about the handsome man. No, she doesn't just find him handsome; she finds him intoxicating, intriguing, and she wants him more than she has anyone. Ever.

"I've seen that look before." Ember's voice is low but filled with humor. "Hell, I've had that look."

Ruby watches as the woman's eyes slide over her husband, who is dangerously handsome with tattoos peeking out from under his shirt.

"Really?" Ruby is interested in that story.

"Oh yes, we met in Paris, and I had planned a wild one-night stand with the ultimate bad boy." She grins and lets her eyes roam over him once again. "But I found I couldn't let him go after." She locks her gaze on Ruby's eyes. "They fight their demons, and it isn't always easy, but they are so worth it. I love Colin, and he needs someone to love him hard. Do you know what I mean?"

Ruby stares at the woman she just met. Love? She didn't even know the man. She was only appreciating his form, his looks, his quiet masculinity, not planning a future.

"Anyway, think about it. I hope we can be friends," she calls back over her shoulder as she walks away and out the door. Ruby doesn't know what to say or even if she could say anything. Stunned into silence. Mark would've said it was impossible.

"Erik asked me to stay." She jumps when Colin speaks so close to her ear. She hadn't heard him. In fact, she had thought he was gone. "Sorry, I didn't mean to scare you."

"I thought you had all left."

"I wouldn't leave without saying thank you. Or without saying goodbye." His voice is soft.

"I'm glad."

"I saw you talking to Ember, so please ignore anything she says." He says it good heartedly, but she can tell he hopes Ember hasn't told her any of his secrets.

"Oh, really. What if she said I should do like she did with her husband?" Ruby smiles, her eyes filled with interest, and it takes his breath.

Bot knows all about how Ember and Carter got together. Carter hadn't told him the details, but he got the picture of how wild those first few meetings were. He swallows, unsure of what he should do. She's sexy as hell, and he'd like nothing more than to take her to bed. But he's more broken than Carter ever was. She doesn't need to be dragged into his nightmare of a life, his violence, or the ugliness of his job.

He's still thinking of how to let her down gently when she turns and her lips caress over his. Soft like silk, warm like the sun, and sweet like honey; all those things run through his mind as she deepens the kiss. He balls his fists at his sides to keep from grabbing her.

She breaks away from him, and they both fight to draw a breath. "I'm not a good man, Ruby."

"I don't believe that, but does it matter today? Right this moment?" She bites at her lip. "You are alone. I am alone. Couldn't we find comfort in each other?"

She feels bold and almost desperate. She didn't tell him she was tired of being alone. That she, too, has ghosts she wants to forget for at least a little while in his arms.

Erik had been telling her about the man he had been working with. She had donated money and gotten others to donate to a charity he had suggested, one she suspects Ember runs with Colin's technical help.

She sees the minute his resolve to leave her alone breaks.

He leans in to kiss her, teasing at the seam of her lips until she opens. He plunges his tongue deep within the heat of her mouth. She pulls back and nibbles at his lips before sucking his full lower one in between her teeth, tugging at it. He groans and his hands run up her bare arms.

Colin knows he shouldn't, but her boldness mixed with the hint of desperation that so matches his own calls to him. He wants to comfort her and maybe in the process, exorcise his own demons for a short while.

She slides her hand down his arm and links their fingers before turning and leading him up the stairs. They go past the rooms she had given him and the others to a set of double doors at the end of the long hall. She pushes the slightly cracked door open with her other hand, and he smiles at the delicate pink polish on her nails. It doesn't seem to match her personality at all.

The room is decadent, and he gets a feel of her true nature here in her actual domain.

"It was my parents, but I had it redone to suit me after I moved into it." She looks at him, judging his reaction.

"It suits you." She smiles at his words.

"The rest of the house I've kept basically the same way it's been for a hundred years, but this one room, I wanted it to be me. Really me, not the me everyone sees."

Colin understands she is giving him something special by letting him in here. It would be like him taking her to his basement, which he realizes sounds completely serial killer-ish and is why he doesn't say it out loud.

Instead, he remains silent as he lets her lead him across to the huge bed draped in midnight-blue fabrics. They are just a slight bit darker than the panels on the walls, which are framed by gold trim. The rest of the walls are so dark, they look almost black, but he can tell they are more like rich chocolate. Decadent. Sinful.

Crystal wall sconces bathe the room in dim golden light, and a velvet couch is against one wall. A chair that matches it is on the other side of the room, but it is the matching bench at the foot of her bed that gives him ideas. An image of her draped over it on her stomach, bared to him, makes his dick even harder than it already was.

As if Ruby could read his mind, she sits on that bench and leans back. The motion causes her back to arch and her breast to push up, begging for his attention.

"I can't offer more than this. Today. Tonight." He gives her one more chance to kick him out of her house and her life.

She doesn't know him and is entirely too good for him but she just smiles.

"Who say I want more, Colin? My life is complicated." She sighs a bit as she waits for him to make his decision once more.

Her blouse, like her pants, is a muted color, something deemed appropriate by the people in her social circle. To help him along, Ruby reaches up, takes the tiny pearl button of her very proper blouse, and slips it through the hole. Then she does the next and the next.

In seconds, as she watches his eyes flare with lust, what she hides underneath those proper clothes begins to be revealed. Bordeaux-colored lace cups her full breasts, the sheerness revealing the duskiness of her nipples. She keeps going until the silk of the blouse slides from her shoulders.

He knows exactly what he's going to do but continues to hold himself still, muscles taut, just watching. He's been to strip clubs, but this is the fucking sexiest thing he's ever seen. She stops as the blouse falls off of her creamy skin.

"The rest." A command. A demand. His voice is guttural, thick with desire. Her eyes flare open, then her lids drift half closed, and she watches him as she complies.

She stands and reaches down to her hip, unzipping her trousers. Turning and giving him her back, she pushes them down over her hips. Her boldness surprises her some, making her glance back. The growl that rumbled in his chest is her reward for that boldness.

"Goddamn, Ruby." That's it, just those two words, but they mean everything to her in that moment. She bends at the waist and shows him even more as she pushes the pants all the way down, then straightens and steps out of them. It leaves her standing in her bra, panties, and a pair of black Louboutins. She waits.

His hand on the middle of her back causes her to flinch, startled, for he hadn't made a sound as he moved close to her. She draws a deep breath, taking him into her lungs. He smells of sweat and forest.

"You are so fucking sexy." His finger runs straight down her spine to the edge of the satin covering her ass, sort of. These panties had a keyhole design, and she swallows hard when that same finger continues down to skim over that bare part of her ass.

Ruby closes her eyes at the rush of sensations. She stays still, eyes closed, as her body comes alive with need. She had wanted him as soon as she saw him, probably even before that, if she was honest, but to feel him touching her feels primal.

It's scary because it is still just one finger skating over her skin. Suddenly, she feels his breath blow over her ear and his voice is low as he whispers to her.

"We have this one day, and I'm going to take my time."

Shit. Her muscles clench, causing a rush of damp heat, and she moans, at a loss for words. Then his touch is gone, and she starts to turn.

"No." He stops her and she freezes, waiting. "Kneel on the bench."

Her breaths become gasps as she moves to comply. He steps in close, forcing her to place her knees wide, opening her. Then his heat is gone once again. Her eyelids flutter as she listens, trying to figure out where he has gone. She hears the sound of clothes being removed, and her heart begins to pound.

Colin tosses his clothes aside, his hand gripping himself tightly as she stands waiting for his touch. Her body trembles, but she stays exactly where she was told. Something about that makes him even hungrier for her. He moves in close again, reaching out and running his palm over the curve of her ass, letting his fingers curl as he drags them down her thighs. She sucks in a breath when he pushes against her thighs, widening them even more, baring even more of her to him.

Goosebumps rush over her skin when he replaces his hands with his jaw, letting his stubble rub over the tender flesh roughly. He plans to take his time, learn every inch of her, every secret hollow and each place that makes her moan.

His hands slide around her thighs and they slip up until

his fingers feather over the lace-covered mound at the junction of those luscious thighs. One hand comes back around, flares out over her narrow waist, and then comes to rest on the small of her back.

He licks the smooth skin right at the bottom of her butt cheek as he applies pressure on her back.

Ruby bends even while her body trembles. As she lays her head against her comforter, she has a crystal clear thought. She will be forever changed after this.

She will be craving him for years to come.

He pulls gently at the lace and satin that hides her core from him, sliding the red fabric down over her ass, leaving it at her knees. Colin rocks back on his heels, just staring at her. Smooth and wet, begging for his touch. Begging him to taste, to devour.

Ruby shifts just a little, nerves stretching tight. The anticipation is eating at her.

Colin feels his control snap with that tiny twist of her hips. She cries out as he lowers his head, licking through her cleft. His tongue strokes over her most sensitive spot, teasing and torturing until her breath is coming in gasps. He backs off, refusing to let her come so quickly.

Ruby cries out, her hips shifting backwards. Seeking more from him. Craving more from him. Demanding more from him.

He moves closer, his lips feathering over her spine as he slides himself over her wetness, teasing her and himself. One hand braces him over her as the other slides around and cups her ample breast, rubbing the nipple through the lace.

She arches her back, thrusting her core back and breast down into his hand. He pinches that nipple harder in response, and she moans. Still, he doesn't enter her. He wants her begging.

She knows what he wants but she isn't one to beg. She

tries to force him into her body, rolling her hips while pushing back. His swollen cock rubs over and over her nub, and she can feel her climax building. Her hips move faster and faster, and she starts to pant.

Colin moves back once again.

"Dammit, Colin, please." She closes her eyes at the plea. Damn him.

Just as the thought slides through her mind, he slams into her. He buries himself so deep that she feels stretched. Her muscles grip at him as he pulls back. The motion is repeated over and over. He straightens and one hand grabs her hip to hold her still for his pounding while the other slides up her spine. He buries his fingers in her fiery hair and jerks her head back, forcing her back to arch even more.

She screams in ecstasy as he sets a punishing pace. The pleasure skitters toward pain, it builds at a furious pace, and when her orgasm crashes through her, she begs again.

She begs for more and for less as another orgasm begins to build immediately. He jerks free of her clenching muscles and flips her over, wanting to see her pleasure, wanting to taste her pleasure.

She is shocked when he lowers his head. His tongue strokes over her, a long deep caress before he sucks on her, swallowing her aftershocks. She cries out and nearly comes off the bed. Her fingers grasp at midnight fabric as she looks down at him staring up her body. Primal lust is etched on his gorgeous face; it is almost sinful how sexy the man looks to her.

Just like that, she is addicted, just like she knew she would be.

He crawls up her body until he is poised over her, his cock nudging at her entrance. She raises up and licks over his lips, and he growls in response. She tastes herself there before he deepens the kiss, devouring her. His hands catch at her hips and lift her, opening her. She locks her eyes on his; his eyes are almost the color of her comforter, dark, almost black with his desire for her. He plunges into her, driving through the swollen muscles, lodging against her womb, once again stretching her as pleasure washes through her.

Colin sets a fast tempo, and the orgasm begins at his feet, burning a fiery path up his legs until it reaches his cock. Her body clamps down on him, and his release erupts, filling her with his seed as her muscles clamp down on him and she screams out her pleasure.

They both struggle to catch their breath as he collapses over her, their body's slick with sweat. He rolls to his side and she stares at the ceiling, unsure what to do now.

She's never done this, never had sex with a man she didn't really know.

"Ruby?" She turns her head to find him watching her. "Do you... Are you..." Colin stops, unsure how to ask.

"It was amazing. More than amazing. I just didn't know if you'd ..." She chuckles. "Jesus, we both suck at this."

He laughs with her. "Come here." He pulls at her, and she rolls into his arms.

CHAPTER NINE

HE HAD HELD HER THROUGH THE NIGHT, WAKING HER A couple times to take her again, and now he lays in the dark, staring at the ceiling, afraid to sleep. Afraid to wake her with screams and flailing arms. His eyes had closed earlier, but the images were there, just like always.

He sighs and slides slowly out from under her arms and the leg she has thrown over him. He stops once he's on his feet and turns to look down at her. Subtle darkness shows under her eyes from her tiredness.

In this moment, he understands why Carter fought so hard to stay away from Ember; he also understands why Carter found himself in foreign cities with her. The peace found in Ruby's arms is the ultimate temptation, but just like his boss, he can't saddle her with his demons.

He walks on silent feet as he picks his clothes up and then makes his way down the hall. Closing the door to the room she had given him just the night before, he heads into the bathroom attached to it, showering quickly so he can make his getaway.

Ruby held her breath until he got down the hall, and then

it escaped with a woosh. She had dozed throughout the night, happy to be awakened by his need and desire. Her body is sore but she will hold the twinges of pain to her as a way to savor him. She had known the last time he took her that he would be gone when she woke. It was why she had fought sleep. She brings her fingers to her swollen lips and touches them lightly, determined not to cry, not in regret or heartache.

Biting her lip, she forces herself to remain quiet and frozen when the bedroom door opens again down the hall. She can see him, the light from the front windows high-lighting him like some avenging angel. He stares at her for one minute then two as she watches him fight his own need. He takes a step forward before spinning away and practically running down her stairs.

"Goodbye, Colin." The words are whispered, her throat tight as she rolls to where he had lain and pulls the covers to her face, dragging in the scent of him. "So stupid, Ruby."

Colin stands with his back against the door, molars grinding together. He wants to punch something, no kill something. What had he been thinking? Even after the shower, he can smell her, taste her. Ruby will just be another ghost to haunt his dreams now. He shakes his head before pushing off the door and stalking through her garden. The sun is up once again, and the morning is turning to day as he steps clear of the vine-covered arch. He shakes his head when he sees Joe standing across the street.

"What are you doing here?" He demands as he stops in front of his friend.

"Nothing." Joe shrugs.

"Nothing?" Colin feels his anger start to spark to life. "You're just standing across the street from Ruby's house for no fucking reason?"

"Just waiting on you, kid." It was the truth. Joe knew

Colin would run, for they all do it. Carter did, but lucky for that asshole, Ember ran him to ground. Joe wonders if the same is about to happen here. He wonders if Ruby is the kind of woman that faces the demons and tames the fuckers.

Ember seemed to think so; that's why she had him standing here all damn night, calling in hourly reports. It's also why she was currently having an early lunch with Erik. Well that, and they are discussing the kids that were rescued, figuring out how to get them all home and the help they will need. But Joe isn't fooled; he saw the look Ember gave Ruby yesterday.

He can't blame her for her hope. She saved Carter and she believes they can all be saved. He might not agree but he does think Colin can be and because of that reason, he stood here and watched. He watched as she kissed him and led him up the stairs. So, maybe she is strong enough to help him.

"You're waiting on me?" Colin's eyes narrow.

"Yep, all night." He grins at the younger man. "You have fun?"

"None of your fucking business," Colin growls as he turns and stalks down the street.

Joe falls into step beside him. "So..."

Colin keeps his eyes forward and doesn't take the bait. He knows Joe has been worried and he also knows Joe has something on his mind. But everyone at Veil Security knows you can't rush Joe; as a matter of fact, if you push him, he will shift even slower.

They walk in silence until they come to a cafe. "Coffee?"

Joe nods and pulls open the door. They order and then sit at a table. Joe lets Colin have the chair in the corner, putting himself between Colin and the small crowd. The entire team needs the safety of it. Joe is no exception but he always lets the others have the security of it. Colin believes it's because Magic isn't just his call sign, it's something he has. Some of the shots Joe made in the war were impossible but he did it. He also handles all the shit they did before so much better.

They all self-medicated -- some with drugs, others with other things like sex or the danger of their job. They all had days that the demons and ghosts won, all except Joe. He was steady. Level. Bot didn't understand how he did it.

If he asked, Joe would tell him all those assumptions and thoughts were complete bullshit. He's not better than the rest of them. Hell, he's probably worse because he hides his shit too well. Joe learned at the hands of his daddy to lock that shit down tight. To hide all your private feelings away.

It was beaten into him at a very young age, and while his grandmother tried to save him from the worst of it, she couldn't save him from it all.

Joe has ghosts from long before the war, and his demon has his father's face.

"So. You wanna tell me why you left your momma's?" Colin shakes his head. He most certainly does not want to talk about his best friend's family walking by the window every fucking day. "Okay, if you aren't ready to deal with that shit, then you aren't. We had hoped being home would help you get some rest at least. Did you sleep any better?"

"Some."

Joe blinks at the one word answer. He remembers Bot the way he was before. He doesn't ever remember being that kind of happy and carefree. He wants it for his friend again.

"Ruby is a beautiful woman," he adds, with a healthy dose of interested speculation in his tone, and locks his face down to keep from grinning at the instant look of white hot jealousy that enters Bot's eyes. "A man could lose himself in her. At least for a few nights." He laughs, and Bot frowns.

"She's not like that."

"Really? Why, because of her fancy house and pedigree? Erik said she was high-falutin'." Bot's eyes narrow.

"Why are you talking about Ruby with Erik?"

"I knew she was a friend of his so I thought I'd see if I had a chance." He shrugs at Bot, who sees red.

"You leave her the fuck alone, Magic. I mean it."

Joe straightens at his anger. "I ain't going to mess with her, but you watch your tone."

Joe hadn't been serious and hell, he had been pushing for a reaction but he didn't like the fact that Bot sounded like he wasn't good enough for the woman.

"Sorry, man, I'm fucked up right now." Bot slumps, placing his arms on the table and leaning his head down on them. "I'm always going to be fucked up. She'd be better off with a man like you."

"Bullshit. I ain't what that fancy lady is looking for, and you might be fucked up, but we all are. If she helps you, helps you get better, then why not go back to her instead of sneaking away in the early morning darkness?"

"It wasn't dark." Joe pins him with a hard glare.

"You and Carter are fucking knuckleheads. I ain't going to drag you kicking and screaming to the water, dumbass. You remember what happened last time."

Bot did indeed. Ember almost died, and they spent months tracking the human trafficker that had seen and shot her. Hell, it's what started all this shit. All because Carter wouldn't admit his feelings. Luckily, Bot never had to see Ruby again. Hell, she didn't know anything about him other than he worked with Erik. Fuck.

He pulls out his phone and hits Erik's contact. The man picks up on the second ring.

"Do not tell her anything else about me. I'm no good for her and I won't drag her into this nightmare of a life."

CHAPTER TEN

ERIK LOOKS DOWN AT HIS PHONE SMILING.

Bot hadn't even let him speak, just growled his threat at him, because it was a threat, and then hung up.

"Who was that?"

He looks up at the two women sitting across from him at the table. He had been here at the hotel restaurant for a couple hours with Ember and then he had sent Ruby a text, and she came right over. Joe had told him the minute Colin had snuck from her house.

Ruby's eyes were locked on his phone, and Ember's were filled with humor. Ember knew exactly who that had been on the call.

"Colin."

"Oh." She doesn't say anything else, but her cheeks went pinker, telling them all they needed to know.

"Can I say something that might be none of my business?" Ember asks, turning her body toward Ruby, and Erik's friend nods. "If you want anything more than a one night-stand, it is going to be hard work. Erik told me about your brother this morning." Ruby jerks her face toward her friend. Erik says nothing; he's tired of Ruby shouldering it all herself. "Bot could be your brother, if he didn't have the whole team holding him barely together. But we aren't enough anymore. He needs help, and so do you. I'll leave you guys to talk, but just one more thing first... I met Carter and I knew after that first night I would never find another man like him. I had a very kind, amazing woman tell me that the love of a man like Carter, like Bot, was worth the fight to get it and keep it. She was right."

Ember stand and comes around the table. Leaning down, she kisses Erik on the cheek. "Thanks again for saving me that night."

He nods and thinks about how one dance had changed so much. If he believed in fate, he'd think it had sent Ember to him in that club in Denver.

"Erik?" He drags his eyes away from Ember's retreating form but not before noticing Carter push off the wall. He hadn't noticed the man before, which says a lot.

"Sorry, Red. What did you say?"

"I said, 'What should I do?'" She has tears pooling in her eyes. "I can't deal with another person disappearing like Mark."

Erik sighs. Maybe this had all been a horrible idea. He had thought that if Bot met Ruby, he might want to help her. No one else had been able to find Mark, not even himself with all his contacts, but Bot was a wizard when it came to finding things and people.

"What happened?" He asks and she gives him the look she has since she hit teenage years, the one that says she thinks he's an idiot.

"You know exactly what happened." Her cheeks color again. "God, Erik, I'm an idiot. I thought one night just to forget for a while but..." She trails off.

"But now you want more." He finishes for her. She nods. "Is it because you couldn't save Mark so you want to save Bot?"

Jesus, she thinks, is that it? Is she trading one train wreck for another? She shakes her head slowly. "I don't know. Honestly. I don't want to hurt him or use him. Maybe we are both too broken."

He knows all about her brokenness and not just the stuff from losing Mark.

"Give it a couple days. Give me a couple of days." She nods, letting the topic die.

Instead, she asks him about his family. Punishment. She knows his family is as messed up as hers. They talk for a while longer before they rise to say goodbye. She hugs him tight, and he squeezes her. She is the closest thing to a sister he'll ever have, and he's going to help her. Somehow.

As soon as they part, he texts Joe. He needs to figure out how to protect her and his friend while getting Bot to try to find Mark. He stays where he is, ordering food while he waits for Joe to arrive. He's pushing the plate away just as the man walks in.

Erik watches him closely. Everyone that knows the security company and the team believe Carter is the leader. They are wrong. Carter is the face, but Joe is the one that keeps it all going. Erik did his research before he started working with Bot and the others. Joe's name is on the incorporation paperwork. Carter even told him that the company had been Joe's idea, a way to help their brothers after they came home.

Carter might be the Alpha of the pack, but Joe is the Beta. He keeps everyone safe while looking out for their well-being. Joe will know what to do about Red and Bot.

Erik isn't surprised when he sees the one they call *Loup,* or wolf, slide into a seat at the bar. The Frenchman had come across his radar before he knew who he worked with. Jacques was a loner, which had made him perfect for his job in the military, but it was his family history that intrigued Erik's bosses. They didn't like that they couldn't tempt him away from Veil Security.

The man nods once while sipping a dark beer, and the foam catches on the massive mustache and beard. The facial hair and the unusual haircut make Jacques look more like an American biker from some television show than the multi-millionaire he actually is. Although, other than his home, as far as Erik can tell, he never touches his family money, other than the recent donations to Ember's charity.

Joe pulls out the chair opposite and sits down. He seems relaxed, but Erik knows he could be ready to kill without any hesitation.

"This is a mess." The man's deep Southern drawl is thick, and like always, Erik takes a moment to decipher the words.

"What is?" He doesn't give away his thoughts on what happened last night or Ruby's reaction to it.

"You know what." The look on Joe's face dares Erik to deny it. "I know exactly why you sent Bot to that *safe house*. He doesn't need anything else to send him spiraling farther down, and if he can't find that girl's brother, that is exactly what will happen. Did she tell you they fucked?"

Erik frowns at the coarseness of Joe's declaration.

"I see she did. Well, what are you going to do about it?"

"What do you think I should do? They are grown, after all. I'm not her keeper, and you aren't his dad," Erik growls, angry at the accusation and guilty because he knows Joe is a least a little right.

"Can he find that man alive?" Joe studies Erik as the man ponders the question.

"If anyone can, it would be Bot. That's why I sent him to her."

Joe shakes his head. "I hope you're right." Sighing, the man glances around before looking back at Erik. Hard. "Don't do anything. If I'm right, and I am, he'll be back at her door before nightfall."

CHAPTER ELEVEN

Bot paces around the hotel room. He had chosen to come to it rather than back to his mom's. He had at least called and talked to her. She didn't have to tell him he had hurt her, for he could hear it in her voice. Scared her again. She made it clear that Joe had told her exactly when he had left.

'Just happened to be around his ass,' his ass; the crazy Cajun was following him. Bot shakes his head at the thought. Stopping once again to look out the window, hating that his eyes immediately turn her direction.

Stupid fucking idea is what he tells himself, turning away, but he glances back before stopping in front of his laptop and looking at the information he has pulled up on her and her family.

Her brother is in the wind. Off grid. Hiding from his demons and the world, breaking her heart. Bank reports show she's spent a small fortune trying to help and then trying to find Mark to no avail. He understands the sadness that she tried to hide from him better now. He also understands why Erik called him. Why her house was the safe house.

Picking up his phone, he calls the man that sent him to her. Erik picks up on the first ring, and Bot knows he's been waiting for this call and wishes he could have lasted longer than the three days he's been counting the minutes of but his patience has snapped.

"She doesn't need another fuck-up in her life, man." He doesn't let Erik speak before he blurts out the very thing he is trying to convince himself of.

"I didn't think of that, Bot. Honestly. I just thought if you met Ruby, you'd want to help her. I've tried to find him but I can't."

Bot rubs his fingers over his tired eyes hard, pushing them back into the sockets, sighing. It says a lot, what Erik just admitted.

"I didn't have any idea that you'd sleep with her." Bot doesn't miss the slight growl of anger coming from Erik, and his spine stiffens.

"That's none of your fucking business," he growls back.

"She's my goddamn business," Erik barks at him, and for the first time, Bot hears him losing the steel grip on his emotions. Interesting. "I love her, Colin."

Rage floods his system at the words. He loves her. Does she love him?

"Like a sister."

Instant regret for the thought of how he could kill Erik multiple ways running through his head. The man sounds heartbroken at her pain. He can live.

"It's killing me not being able to help her. Hell, I can't even help my best friend."

Bot sighs, trying to imagine losing one of his friends to their demons. He can't. It was hard enough losing his friend to the enemy, something tangible, but to have him just disappear would kill him. The not knowing would eat away at him.

"Fine, but don't tell her. I'll do what I can to find him and whatever I find, I'll send to you."

Erik smiles. "You don't want to get it to her yourself?"

"No." Bot hangs up before Erik can say anything else to piss him off.

Within moments his phone chimes, alerting him to a new message. He opens it and sees Erik has sent him all the files on Mark. He knows he needs to get to his system at home but he can't stand to leave London. He won't admit that it's her that he doesn't want to leave.

Shaking his head at his own stupidity, he pulls up the contact information for the guy who gets him things when he's in the country. It takes him minutes to send the shopping list and where to deliver it all. It'll take a day or so for the guy to get it all together.

Bot looks at himself, reflected in the glass of the window. He hates the man staring back at him. Time to face his mother. Time to face his past.

CHAPTER TWELVE

HE SITS IN THE RENTED CAR JUST DOWN THE STREET FOR hours, feeling like a coward and an idiot. Every person that has passed has smiled and waved; by now, his mother has known he's here since almost the moment he parked.

He starts the car and drives slowly down to his mom's driveway, pulling in and turning it off. He sits for another minute before forcing himself to get out. As he straightens and closes the door, he hears her.

Not his mother.

"Hello, Colin." He grinds his molars as panic flares in his chest.

"Mrs. Ashwood." He turns slowly to look his best friend's mother in the eyes, unable to ignore her any longer.

"We've missed you." She steps forward but stops at an arm's length. "Are you well?"

"Yes. I'm sorry."

She shakes her head, a sad smile curving her lips as she reaches for his cheek with the hand she had cupped her own son's cheek with so often.

Before.

"Nothing that happened was your fault, Colin. Nothing."

He sees that she means it, but that doesn't change his guilt.

"I..." He pauses trying to think of anything to say, anything that would mean enough. "I wish it had been me."

There. It is the truth, and he's thought it every single day since he held her son in his arms as he died. Colin swallows and fight the tears that want to pour down his face. His emotions are choking him as she drags him into a tight hug. No. It's more than a hug; it is a mother holding a son.

It breaks him.

They stand clutching each other, sobbing on the sidewalk as passersby look on. No one says a word; everyone knows who both the people holding so tightly to each other are. More than one person passes with tears shining in their eyes.

The community lost two sons on that day in Afghanistan.

They break apart when they are both cried out. His best friend's mom walks him to his own, who is waiting in the front garden. Neither say anything as they share their own hug. Colin waits, both women holding onto him as if afraid he will once again disappear.

Finally, James' mother pulls away. Once more she cups his cheek, smiling at the boy she helped raise.

"We love you, Colin. Come back and see us," she whispers as she turns away.

He nods once, unable to promise something he's not sure he can do. He refuses to hurt her any more than she has been. His own mom leads him in the house.

"I hope it helped." He looks at her but doesn't answer the unasked question. "Both of you. Carter called to let me know you might be staying for a bit before you head back to the U.S."

"I figured Joe had told you every detail of what I've been

doing and what he thinks I might do." His voice sounds grumpy, even to him, and she smiles.

"They don't want me to worry." It is a quiet scolding from her. A reminder that he snuck out in the middle of the night, making her do exactly that.

"I'm sorry," he sighs, putting his arm around her shoulders. "I'm sorry for everything -- the last few years, the last few days. I'm sorry I don't call or visit. I'm sorry I've made you worry so much."

"I love you, and it's my job to worry. I started the moment I felt you growing in me and I will only stop when I leave this world." She lays her head against his chest, listening to his heart beat. "I just want you to come home from that battlefield."

"I am home, mom."

She shakes her head against him. "No, you aren't. You are still right there, holding James on your lap, screaming for help. But now you need to help yourself. James is beyond saving, Colin. You have to save yourself."

He doesn't respond because once again, he can't promise that.

CHAPTER THIRTEEN

Ruby looks around her home. A home that she has loved since she was little, but now it is filled with ghosts, ghosts of a life she can barely remember. It reminds her of a life she can't have.

It reminds her of death, so much death it chokes her. She doesn't know how to live anymore. Only in his arms did she feel herself come to life.

She shakes her head, wishing she could forget those moments beneath his body. She scoffs at herself, not believing her own thought for a moment. She will hold the memories tight, letting them give her a small amount of happiness for as long as they will.

She had hoped for the first couple of days that he might return. She had hoped selfishly to steal a few more hours of happiness before returning to her lonely existence. Her friends couldn't understand. She only had Erik, and he was gone for days, weeks, hell, sometimes months.

Day and night, she is alone, even when surrounded by people. Friends laughing and having a good time while she plasters a fake smile on her face. Everyone is tired of hearing about Mark. No one wants to talk about her parents dying. No one understands.

Her phone rings and she glances at it, frowning. She doesn't recognize the number, but it is from the United States. Could it be him? She hates that she thought it immediately.

But she can't help but answer.

"Hello?" She holds her breath, waiting to hear who answers.

"Ruby? I hope you don't mind me calling. I just wanted to check on you."

Ruby lets her breath out slowly as she hears Ember's voice. "Of course not. I'm happy to hear from you. Did the woman and children get to safety?"

"In the process still, for a few of them. Some didn't want to go home. I don't think their homes were safe either, from what we could gather. But we are finding places for them."

"Good. Did you need anything else?" Ruby tries not to sound short, the picture of English manners, but she honestly doesn't understand Ember's reason for checking on her.

She has been cranky for days and really doesn't feel like dealing with anyone, let alone a practical stranger.

"I don't mean to bother you," Ember pauses, and Ruby feels awful. "When I met Carter, I had planned just one night with him. One amazing, wild night of abandon." Ember laughs but Ruby can hear the hint of sadness in her voice and immediately wonders about how they ended up together.

"It didn't work out the way you wanted?" Ruby asks when the woman pauses once again.

"It worked out the way it was meant to be. I knew after that first night I would never be the same, I would never want to be without him."

Now, her voice is filled with love. Ruby is shocked at how

her heart tightens in her chest, her entire body filled with longing and not a small amount of jealousy at it.

"How did you know?" Ruby's voice shakes with her fear.

Fear that she has already missed her opportunity. An image of Colin, sleeping in her bed, his hair covering one eye, face relaxed and young looking. Could you love someone after just one night?

"My heart broke as I flew home. I had no way to reach him. I heard nothing for a very long time, and then he met me in another city. After sharing a few days, I decided I couldn't let him go. So I went to him. I risked everything but I gained more than I could have ever dreamed."

Ruby wants that, more than she could dream.

"What are you saying exactly?"

Ember laughs. "I'm saying don't let Colin get away. He will try because he's just like Carter. They think they are saving us but in reality, they are just terrified of hurting us. Their demons ride them hard some days, but a very wise woman once told me that because of that, they love hard. And that kinda love is worth everything."

To be loved hard sounds amazing.

"I don't even know if that's possible, keeping him. I don't even know how to get in touch with him. I don't even know if he's still in England."

"Oh, he's in England. Today, he's at his mom's. She just messaged me, letting me know that he was finally facing some of those demons that are riding him hardest."

Ember doesn't elaborate, for that's Colin's story to share. She just hopes he does.

"Listen, he's staying at Park Grand, if you want to go find him. I'm not sure which room. I'll let you know when he's headed back to the city."

"Why are you helping me?" Ruby inquires as she takes her stairs two at a time.

"Because I've seen your face before, when I looked in a mirror. I've seen the one Colin was wearing on Carter's. It takes a special person to love someone like them. I believe you are that kind of special. I hope you don't mind, but Erik told me about your brother. I think you can help each other."

Ruby tenses at her words. She feels a sense of anger at Erik for sharing her personal business.

"It's fine." Her voice doesn't sound a bit like it's okay, but Ember doesn't comment on it. "I'd appreciate any help you can give me."

She has adopted her posh accent, the one that locals know mean she is distancing herself from them. Ember doesn't recognize the change or is choosing to ignore it.

"Great. Call me if you need anything. I do mean anything. Joe will help, I'm sure. I mean, I haven't asked but he will. Okay, I'll let you go. Remember to call me."

"I'll wait for your message." She starts to hang up but instead continues, "Thank you, Ember."

"No problem. I really hope we can become friends." Ruby can imagine the dark-haired woman grinning.

She hangs up without responding, something inside unwilling to let anyone else in, not willing to let her heart be hurt even more. The 'friends' she has are not and have never been true friends. They hold no access to her true self.

If she's honest with herself, she hadn't been herself with anyone for most of her life. Except that night. That night, she bared more than her flesh.

She takes a bag out while standing in her huge closet, a room filled with the armor she wears to protect herself from the social backstabbing and ladder-climbing. Gowns and suits, silly hats and jewels, the armor of a woman of her standing, passed down from mothers to daughters.

She ignores it all and instead pulls things she wears to bring her happiness, things that soothe her soul. An old sweater of Mark's, comfortable jeans, t-shirts, and then she throws more things in before striding out.

It only takes her minutes until she's out the door and driving toward the hotel. She lets the valet park her car and strides in, just like her mother taught her. She stops in front of the registration desk and smiles cooly at the man standing there.

"You have a guest staying here; his name is Colin Martin. I want the room next to him." Her brow raises when he doesn't respond immediately.

"I'm sorry. I can't say if we have a guest by that name. Our guest's privacy is our utmost concern."

She smiles again. "Does Jonathan still own this beautiful establishment?" She pulls out her phone and scrolls through her contacts, tapping one while keeping the cool smile on her face. "Hello. I'm at the hotel. If I hand the man my phone, can you help me get the room I want?" She listens as the man in question's eyes grow large. "Of course, darling. I just wanted to get away from the house and get some pampering. Yes, of course. Tonight at eight would be wonderful. Just a moment."

She holds out her phone the man takes it his hand shaking a bit. "Hello?"

Ruby fights the laughter that threatens to bubble up as Jonathan lets the man know she better be in the room she asked for within minutes.

"Of course, sir. I'm sorry, sir." He hands the phone back and waves his hand at a bellman. "Take Miss Chadwick to room six-oh-one. Your key, miss, and I'm sorry for the delay and inconvenience. If there is anything, I mean anything, you require, just call."

She follows the man up to her room and then closes the door, leaning against it. Dinner at eight, but she needs to get something from home to wear. Sighing, she pushes away from the door, goes to where the man had left her bag, and starts to pull her things out.

Then a diabolical thought enters her mind. Ruby's hands stop in midair, her shirt hanging from them. The look on her face is one every woman has worn at least once in her life. The look that says she knows how to get exactly what she wants.

The shirt falls forgotten as she moves around the bed and sits. Pulling out her phone, she finds the call from this morning and then picks up the receiver from the hotel phone and dials.

"Hello?" Ember cautiously answers.

"Ember, it's Ruby."

"Oh, hi. Nothing is wrong, is it?" Her voice instantly changes from cautious to concerned.

"No. No, I'm fine. I just have an idea and I wonder if you could help."

"Do tell."

Ruby smiles at the excitement in the other woman's voice and she does just what Ember asks. She lays out her plan to hopefully get Colin for herself. When she finishes, Ember is giggling gleefully.

"I'll make sure he's there." She laughs again and says two more words before hanging up. "Good luck."

Ruby is pretty sure she's going to need it to pull it all off. She grabs her purse and leaves the room.

Time to make him squirm.

CHAPTER FOURTEEN

It's getting dark when he reaches the hotel. He had planned to come back today anyway, but Ember's call had caused him to leave his mom's house earlier than he had planned.

She had seemed worried, distracted even, not like herself. So, here he was parking his car so he can go up and get the computers set up.

He's almost to the elevator when he hears a tinkling laugh. It stops him in his tracks, and he glances back over his shoulder, eyes roaming the lobby. Flaming red hair shimmers in the chandelier lights, and he turns slowly.

Her body is covered in slinky sapphire fabric that shows her every curve, and the back is cut low, showing the expanse of her back, which is currently being gently caressed by some asshole's perfectly groomed hand.

Colin fights the urge to stomp across the lobby and snap the fingers that just glided up her spine. Her own fingers play across the man's expensive suit for a moment before she pulls them back.

Colin bristles when she lets the guy guide her into the dining room.

"What the fuck?" He mumbles as he frowns.

He looks around, trying to find Joe or any of the others. He sees no one. Why this hotel? He had told no one, except his computer guy, and he doesn't know him well enough to know anything about her.

Does he?

He looks around again, but his eyes return to her. He walks to the maitre d and asks him for a table for one. He then guides him to a table in a dark corner with a clear view of her. As he sits, he asks the man about the beautiful couple.

"That is the owner and his friend," the man offers without pausing. Idiot.

"They look happy." The man smiles then hands him the menu as he turns away.

They do, and he wants to punch the guy's perfect teeth right out of his perfect face. He is everything Colin can't be.

Colin mumbles under his breath, "Fuck."

He watches as they eat and laugh, wishing he could hear what they are saying. He loves the joy he sees on her face at moments, although it is fleeting.

They don't notice when he follows them out. He watches the elevator and sees it stop on his floor. Taking the stairs three at a time, he is there in time to see them enter the room next to his.

Another coincidence?

He opens his door and closes it silently. Listening with his ear against the wall, he can hear the muffled sounds of them talking. Then it grows quiet and his heart pounds.

He listens for a few more moments before forcing himself to turn away, noticing his new system sitting waiting for him to use it, and he does. He searches for the man, he searches her background. Only when he finds the information he's looking for does his heart start to slow, does his jealousy begin to ease.

His eyes glance back at the wall separating them. Jealousy. He's never felt it before. He doesn't like the feeling. Not one bit.

He has no reason to at the moment. The man is no threat. A friend. Barely. He owns the hotel, a friendly dinner with a woman he's known for many years. Nothing more. The man is very lucky that it's nothing more.

But he still can't pull his eyes away from the wall.

The soft strains of music begins to filter through the wall. It makes him wonder for a moment. She had a night with him. Is she looking for a night with another?

Sliding his phone from his pocket, he scrolls until he sees the number he's looking for.

When the call is answered, he speaks immediately. "Tell me about Jonathan."

"Bot?"

Bot imagines Erik wiping his hands over his face.

"Jonathan who owns the hotel."

"He's a friend of ours. He has been since we were kids. He has an interest in Ruby, but she's never felt the same. Why?" His friend sounds genuinely surprised and interested.

"I saw them eating dinner here at the hotel. He is in her room, as we speak. A room that is right next to mine."

"Umm, okay. Well, I didn't expect that. What do you want to do?"

Bot sighs. That is the question, isn't it? "I don't know." That was a lie. He knew exactly what he wanted to do. "I've told you I'm no good, especially not for her."

"Yes, you've said that, but would you say the same about Joe or Jacques if they found a woman that might be the one?"

He feels the denial boil up before Erik can even finish. He would want nothing but happiness like Carter found with

Ember for all of his brothers. The problem is he is much worse than the others. He's tried to hide it, but the intervention said that he'd done a piss poor job.

"That's your answer, Bot. Why not give her a chance? I know you had computers delivered. I know you plan to find Mark for her. You could also try to find yourself for her."

Erik hangs up before Bot can respond. He is left with his thoughts, and they run rampant through his mind. Before he realizes it, he's up and almost to the door before he stops himself. He stands there, looking back and forth, unsure what to do.

He hears the door next door open and close. His eye is glued to the peephole, watching the man in question move tensely down the hall. Didn't go well, then. The thought makes Bot grin.

He doesn't know what she's doing, but she is up to something. Bot forces himself to turn away from the door and makes his way back to the computers. Lacing his fingers together, he flexes them before placing them on the keyboard.

For hours, the room is silent except for the clacking of keys as he digs deeper and deeper into Mark's trail, searching for her answers.

The sun is high in the sky when his fingers finally stop. Nodding, he pushes back and then stands. Turning away from the screens, he walks to the bathroom. The water is hot in seconds, steam filling the air, fogging the mirror. He strips and steps under the scalding water, letting it cascade over him. He stays there until the knots in all his muscles start to ease.

Knocking at the door forces his head up, and turning off the water, he steps out and wraps a towel around his waist. The gun on the sink slides into his hand easily. He opens the door slightly and then exhales as bright green eyes lock onto his.

"Ruby."

She smiles at the sound of her name on his lips. "Colin."

"What are you doing here?"

"Here at the hotel or here at your room?" She leans against the door frame since he hasn't invited her in.

"Both."

He looks practically edible, the water drops still sliding down his barely golden skin. Her eyes slide over his chest and down stalling at the deep v at his hips. Dark hair curls around his belly button and then travels down beneath the snowy towel.

"Ruby."

She looks up and smiles at his exasperated look.

"The hotel, a friend owns it, and I needed a couple nights away from the house. You saw us last night." She raises a brow. "At dinner. Downstairs."

She likes the look that moves over his face. The surprise that she had noticed him.

"You saw me." A statement, not a question, but she nods in affirmation. "Did you know I was here?"

She shrugs.

"They need to stay out of my business," he murmurs as he opens the door, letting her in. "Have a seat. I'll get dressed." He steps away from her to grab the jeans he had left laying on the bed. "I was going to come to you later."

"Why?" She leans back against the bed while he debates what to tell her.

He watches her while making up his mind. He doesn't look at the computers; he decides to wait until he can confirm the information he found.

"I was going to ask if Joe sent you." She shakes her head in denial. "Erik?"

Again, she shakes her head, and he frowns.

"Does it matter?" She looks at him closely before continuing, "I haven't stopped thinking about you. I've tried but I can't." She holds up her hand even before he opens his mouth to argue. "I've lost every person I love. I've refused to let anyone else get close, fearing they will disappear too. You are the first person I thought might be able to stay. The first I thought might be strong enough. The first I hoped would be."

She stays reclined as he stares at her. He sees hope in her jewel-like eyes. He feels his own sputter to life.

"I'm not sure what you want from me."

She nods at his words, understanding. "I don't know that. I just know that I don't want to not try to find out."

Colin sighs, "I can only disappear." He hates that it is the truth. "I am no better than the others that have left you. I will only break your heart."

"Fine. Then I want another night to forget, another night to hold close when I'm alone." Her fingers move up to the pearl buttons holding the silk of her shirt closed. "Will you give me that? Can I give it to you?"

His eyes are locked on her fingers, on the dove gray polish covering her perfectly manicured nails.

"I can't promise anything more," he warns as he takes a step toward her.

Courage, Ruby. Courage.

She licks over her bottom lip before drawing it between her teeth.

"I wouldn't ask you to." She holds out one of those perfectly manicured hands. She waits patiently until he takes it then she pulls him down to her.

He lets her. He lets her take his lips and then he takes over.

Every ounce of desire he's felt and tried to ignore over the last couple weeks surges up. He pours into her, thrusting his tongue deep into the velvet heat of her welcoming mouth. He clings to her, like the life raft she is offering to be.

The thought makes him pull back and look into her eyes, where he sees the same desire and something else. It's something he doesn't recognize immediately but it touches his soul. She pulls him back, and he lets her, letting go of the feelings battling within him.

Raising up, she crashes into him, losing herself in the velvet heat of his mouth. It makes her moan, and his hand moves to her hair, tightening in it to pull her head back, giving him deeper access. They kiss until they are panting. Her eyes travel down slowly, stopping to watch his muscles flex and ripple.

They get stuck on the vee at his waist for a while before finally landing on her fingers where they've slid under the edge of the denim. She pauses before reaching for the button at the top of his zipper.

He takes over, pushing her hand out of the way.

"I have dreamed of your pussy for a month. The taste. The feel. I feel like I'm starving, Ruby." His voice is husky, and she shivers at the promise in his words.

Moisture soaks her panties as her core clenches. He places his hand flat on her chest and pushes her back. Slower than she'd like, he moves back, standing at the end of the bed and reaching down to unbutton her pants. She gasps when he grips her waistband, yanking them down over her legs.

His lips trail after them, kissing his way to her ankle. Then he starts the slow, agonizing return. Ruby's skin twitches, heated and sensitive, as his teeth scrape over her inner thigh, and his hands slide under her hips, lifting her for his plunder. When he hesitates, she looks down her body at him; he is staring up at her.

The raw hunger and possessive look on his face steals

Ruby's breath. His gaze holds hers as he slowly runs his finger down her cleft to gather her juices on it before bringing it to his mouth, curling his tongue around it. She shivers with need as he separates her folds, leaning slowly forward, eyes still locked on hers as he takes her into his mouth.

She cries out at the sheer pleasure. He closes his eyes, moaning, and it reverberates through her, adding a new pleasure. His tongue slides around and in, over and over. He pauses his assault and then bites down gently on her clit, and she gasps as he thrusts a finger deep inside of her. Slowly, he drags it out and then repeats the process over and over, all while his tongue works over her clit. He adds another, stretching her, and her body tightens.

She pants his name while her hips undulate, trying to find release. Higher and higher, he pushes her, all the while holding her body in place. Ruby's toes curl as her orgasm builds, fire streaking up her legs and over her belly. Then it hits her like a bomb, crashing over her, wave after wave of ecstasy so fierce and overwhelming, she throws her head back and screams, not caring who hears.

Sweat glistens on her skin as Bot rises from devouring her. He pushed her over the edge multiple times and lapped up every bit of cream her pussy gave him, and still he's hungry for her. Her eyes are dazed, and she holds her hand out to him, beckoning him to come to her.

Bot prowls up her body, licking and biting a path to her heaving breasts. Her soft mewls urge him on. Her eyes stay locked on his as he draws her hardened nipple into his mouth. Her back arches, pushing them closer. Bot releases it with a wet pop.

Raising up, he grabs her thighs and pushes her legs up, opening her for his view. Her breath catches as she raises up on her elbows and watches as Bot slides into her. He goes slow, savoring it inch by long, full inch until he's filling her completely. She moans as he reaches the end, reaching for him, trying to force him deeper. He stops and grabs her hands, stretching them above her head and shifting to hold them with one hand. She tries to pull free, and Bot growls, his free hand wrapping in her hair. He slides out, leaving just the tip in. Watching her closely, he plunges deep and hard. Over and over, he repeats the motion, until she is crying his name. The sound of it on her lips pushes him harder. Her heels dig into Bot's ass, pushing him harder, begging him for more.

Bot releases her hands, but she clutches the pillow, fighting to hold them where he'd put them. Pushing up, he pulls her hips higher, changing the angle so he can watch as he fucks her, his fingers hard on her hips. Her body starts to shudder, gripping him in molten velvet. Bot drives his cock into her, over the sensitive bundle of nerves, stretching the swollen folds, pushing her to the edge again. Her hands fly to his shoulders, her nails digging in as she rolls her hips and tightens those muscles even more.

"Fuck, Ruby," he hisses.

She doesn't stop, just continues to impale herself on his cock. His breath explodes out of his lungs, and he grips one of those undulating hips in a punishing grasp before leaning over and taking her mouth in a brutal kiss. It is her only warning. Bot thrusts like a jackhammer, impaling her over and over, driving deep and sending her to the edge of pain. He swallows her cries then breaks the kiss as he feels his release racing through his body. Bot roars her name and slams home, filling her with his thick, hot semen. Her own orgasm tears through her once more, and her body quivers and quakes beneath his.

He collapses on her, and she holds him close as they rock against each other, drawing out the pleasure. He closes his eyes.

I'm fucking screwed; I will never get over this woman. She will always be under my skin. I will always see her face etched with ecstasy.

He raises his head to look down at her, and she smiles before bringing her mouth to his. The kiss is soft and slow. She takes her time, moving over his lips before letting her head fall back.

She struggles to catch her breath even as her heart pounds and sweat trickles down her neck pooling in the divot at the base of her neck. The weight of him on top of her is both crushing and delicious. He is also struggling to catch his breath, his hand continuously moving over her hot skin.

The feel of it makes her smile, even while she feels the first hint of sadness. Sadness that he is still determined to walk away, that she can feel him pulling away even as he still touches her.

"You take my breath," he murmurs against her chest.

You take my heart, she thinks as she runs her fingers through his damp hair.

His head raises and he locks his eyes on her face. "Are you okay?" She smiles at his sudden concern.

"I'm better than okay. That was amazing. You were amazing." She kisses his forehead, the only thing she can reach. "It was everything I have been dreaming of since the last time."

He raises up on his arms, drawing closer to her face, studying her.

Courage, Ruby. Stick to the plan. A plan she had made like any soldier going to battle. She has to take advantage of his weakness. So, she does just that. She kisses him deeply and long enough to stir his desire once again before breaking away. She turns her eyes to where she knows the clock sits, ignoring the computers, although she does wonder if he is already on another job. Hunting.

"Oh goodness, it's late. I really have to go." She pushes at him, then swings her still trembling legs over the edge of the bed. "I have an appointment with Jonathan. If I don't hurry, I'll miss it completely." She grabs her clothes, pulling them on quickly, making her way to the door as he sits staring at her. Shock and confusion are clouding his eyes.

This is it.

She looks back as she pulls the door open. "If you are ever back in London..." She smiles before walking out. Three long steps and she is at her own door, which she leans against when she closes.

She glances at the shared wall before crossing to the bathroom. She closes the door and turns on shower before dialing her phone.

"How'd it go?" Ember voice sounds so hopeful.

"I'm not sure. Can you meet me somewhere?" Ruby feels strange asking this woman she hardly knows, but no one else might understand.

"Of course. Joe was my co-conspirator; he might be able to give us some ideas on how to push Bot's button, which is really what I had to do with Carter. Well, that and I got shot, but let's try not to do that this time."

Shot.

Ruby shakes her head, her eyes wide. Did she really want to have the kind of life where she could get shot? An image of those kids' faces pops in her head, followed closely by Colin.

Yes. She wants both.

"I'll send you the address. I can be there in forty-five minutes."

"See you soon." Ember lets out a sigh of relief as she hangs up, and Ruby realizes that she had taken longer to answer than she thought.

She showers and gets ready quickly but takes time to look as good as she can, just in case he is watching as she leaves. Sexy to remind him of who she is supposedly meeting.

Time to plan the next attack.

CHAPTER FIFTEEN

SHE HAD JUST LEFT. BOT HAD STARED AT THE DOOR FOR longer than he cares to admit. Now, he finds himself watching her walk down the hallway to the elevator. Snug black skirt with those stockings that have the line down the back. Golden heels on her feet, highlighting the muscle at her calf, a calf that had been wrapped around him less than an hour ago and now it is carrying her to another man. The dark gold shirt clings to her waist and wrist but has wide upper arms, making him think of a bygone era. Even her hairstyle harkens to the old movies his mom loves so much.

That's it. She reminded him of those famous actresses, like Garbo and Hepburn. Slightly out of reach, untouchable, somewhere far above him.

And yet she had offered him the happily ever after.

He pushes away long after the elevator doors close. To taste heaven with her and have to give it up was a torture he might not be able to survive.

Shaking his head, he goes to take another shower. In minutes, he's out and dressed. He grabs the information he had written down and heads down stairs.

His eyes narrow when he hits the lobby floor and sees Jacques sitting on one of the tiny uncomfortable chairs, a French newspaper in his hands.

"What are you doing here?" He growls as he stops in front of his friend.

"Waiting for you." The man shrugs, like it had been a stupid question.

"How did you even know I was here?"

The look he gives Bot silently asks if he really wants him to answer.

"Fine. Let's go. I'm assuming you have a vehicle."

"Oui, but of course."

Of course. He stands and Bot is reminded of how much he moves like a predator, silent, stealthy. Bot hadn't worked with him on many missions but he had heard the stories. Jacques was a straight up killer who likes close combat. He didn't want to kill a man from a thousand yards out; he wanted to be looking in your eyes when he shoved the blade between your ribs.

Bot falls in beside the man, letting him lead the way. He raises his brow at the Audi RS7 sitting right outside the hotel entrance. The valet hands him the keys and takes the huge tip for keeping it close. It is sleek and black and reminds Bot of a predator, just like its owner.

"Where are we going?" The Wolf, as the whole team calls Jacques, asks, and the question pulls him from his assessment of the man.

"I have a lead on the woman's brother but I don't want to give her false hope, so we are going to go check it out first. Head north on the M1, and it'll take us three or four hours to get there. Still want to go?"

The man shrugs, rarely saying much more than absolutely necessary, and pulls out onto the road and heads north. They drive in silence for hours.

"So..."

Bot looks over at Wolf. The man is stroking his massive beard, and his eyes flick towards Bot, waiting for an answer to the question he didn't even ask.

"I don't know. I'm no good for her or anyone." Bot looks out the window at the landscape flying by.

"We would disagree with your worth to us." He pauses then continues, "It could be like Ember did for Carter."

Bot thinks of how his boss has changed over the past year. The shadows are still in his eyes, but he is steadier. More solid. He turns to Wolf and studies him for a minute.

"What if it were you?"

"Me? I'm too far gone. I think I started too far even before the war, before the killing." He glances at Bot. Bot sees the ghosts floating there in the man's eyes.

He wonders once again about the Wolf's childhood, but the man looks back at the road, and Bot can feel his walls fortifying.

"Exit here." Bot points out the window, and Wolf sees a sign for North York Moors National Park. He raises a brow. "Instagram post from a hiker had a man in the background trying not to be seen, but my facial recognition software, or the FBI's software, pegged that man with an eighty-nine percent chance of being her brother. So..."

"It's more than you've had before. We'll find this guy and we watch him until your lady gets there. We won't let him slip away."

Bot shakes his head at the excitement on Jacques face. They are all adrenaline junkies, and apparently watching him hadn't been giving the Wolf his hit. He is going to love hunting this guy. Bot just hopes it's actually Mark.

The miles click by as the men fall back into silence. Finally they reach the small town that sits right in the middle of the national park. Wolf parks the car, and they both climb out, the doors shutting with almost silent snicks. Hikers and tourists mill around the street and shops that line it.

The men glance at each other, and then Bot nods left. Wolf knows he will take the right side of town. He walks to the back of the car, pushing the button for the trunk release, and reaches in to pull out a backpack. Bot smirks. If he thinks that is going to make him blend in, he's insane.

A wolf in sheep's clothing.

They search for hours but find nothing. Sitting at a small cafe, they drink tea while trying to decide what to do.

"I'm telling you, the guy scared the fuck out of me," the American in line grumbles at his friend.

Bot and Wolf lock eyes.

"One second, I was standing there trying to take a picture, and the next, he was there. Just fucking materialized out of the trees. Looked like a goddamn Sasquatch. He just stared at me. Then POOF. Gone."

"Jesus, man, what did you do?" The other guy asks, clearly not believing his friend.

"You know what I did, asshole. I ran. I don't give a shit if you think I'm lying. I ain't getting killed like some chick in a horror movie or some idiot on a crime show." The guy shakes his head and glances out toward the north.

Bot unfolds the hiking map he had picked up while he had searched the city. Wolf leans close as they look. Only one hiking trail out that way.

Wolf pulls a laptop from his bag and hands it to Bot. It takes him only minutes to gain access to a satellite. Thirty minutes later, they see what they are looking for. A tiny out of place shelter, mostly hidden. Mark is living off the grid, if it is him.

"Time to take a look." Bot closes the laptop and pushes his chair back.

"We need to be very careful. He's either going to run or

fight. We don't want either."

"We just go close enough to confirm it's him, and then I'll call Erik."

"It'll be dark soon. If it's him, we need to pull back and call the others in. Carter can get them here quickly. We surround the area, just in case," Wolf's voice says Bot doesn't have any say.

"He's not a terrorist," Bot argues.

"No. He's a brother who needs our help before he hurts someone, and we can't do this alone." Wolf's dark eyes narrow, waiting to see if Bot will argue.

He doesn't, and they both move to the the car to grab supplies that Bot isn't surprised he has. It only takes a couple minutes for them to be ready and start toward the trail.

They move quickly and in silence through the trees. Wolf tracks all the signs, although there aren't many. Whoever is living out here is definitely trying to stay off the radar. Suddenly, Bot hears a noise that didn't come from nature and he freezes. Wolf does the same, and they both listen for the sound to come again. It doesn't, so they begin to move again but they are both on high alert.

Bot feels like they have become the prey on this hunt. He glances over at Wolf, and the man nods his agreement. His hand comes up, signaling that they should split, and then he moves away, disappearing into the trees like a ghost.

It only takes a few minutes for Bot's theory to be proved correct. A click sounds right behind Bot, and he freezes. Fuck. Just that word races through his head.

"Who are you?" A voice that sounds like it isn't used much is right behind him.

"My name is Colin." Bot raises his hands out from his body.

"You need to lower that weapon," Wolf's disembodied voice calls out. "Lower it, or I will drop you."

"I'd listen to him," Bot says quietly. "He is like a phantom and likes to use a knife."

"I said who are you and why are you here?"

"Like I said, I'm Colin, and I'm looking for a man named Mark."

The man narrows his eyes as they quarter the darkness around him. "Why?"

"Ruby." Bot doesn't say anything else.

"Fuck. Bloody fucking hell, I asked… No, I told her not to look for me."

Colin draws a deep breath as he hears the gun being slid into a holster. Turning slowly, he looks at the man and could easily understand the American's Sasquatch comment.

"She didn't send me or even ask me." Bot looks around for Wolf, but the man is still hidden. "She is just…"

The angry man standing just inches from him grins. "Yeah, that sounds like my sister. You poor, dumb bastard." He just shakes his head before stepping away.

"Sounds about right." Bot grins back at him. "She's just broken. Lost. Alone. Worried about you."

"I can't. I just can't. I could hurt her or worse." He studies Bot. "Of course, she managed to find someone just like me." He turns away, and Bot falls into step beside him.

"We aren't together. I just wanted…" What did he want? He had no idea. That's a total lie. "I just wanted to help her." He puts his hand on Mark's arm. "To help you, if I can."

"No helping me." He glances around, still searching for Wolf. "I'm too far gone."

"Erik introduced me to Ruby. I work with him some. My brothers and I have a private security company. We help each other. I'm not going to force anything, just putting the offer out there."

He can see the instant denial in the man's eyes, can see his desire to fade away into the darkness.

"Wolf, come out, man," he calls out, and the man in question appears like a spirit from the trees.

"Come on. My place is right over here." Mark points and they notice the shelter. It is a textbook evasion shelter right from training school, totally blending into the surroundings.

They slip inside and sit on the makeshift chairs.

"I called Carter," Wolf says while making sure he is closest to the exit, not giving Ruby's brother a chance to run.

"I'm not going back." Mark tenses, staring into Wolf's dark eyes.

"Didn't say you are."

"She just wants to know that you are alive," Bot offers. "She doesn't think you'll come back. I know you can't, at least not right now. Maybe never. But she deserves some answers. You are killing her slowly."

"I thought you just met her." Mark studies Bot, looking every bit the big brother he is.

"I care about her." Wolf chuckles at Bot's words. "Shut up, asshole."

"So if you care about her so much, why aren't you with her?"

"Too much like you, I guess." Bot shrugs.

"She deserves better than us both."

Bot nods. That she does.

"Maybe she could come here, meet you in town," Wolf offers, causing Mark to look around his shelter.

"She won't care about any of this; she just wants to see you."

Mark nods but still looks like a wild animal about to bolt. "I can't hurt her again, can't hurt her anymore."

The two men watching him ignore the tears they hear in his voice and the demons in his eyes.

Minutes later, the sounds of a helicopter shatter the silence.

CHAPTER SIXTEEN

MARK'S JAW CLENCHES AND UNCLENCHES IN ANGER AND fear.

"What did you do?"

"I told you I called the others." Wolf shrugs. "They are here. You can run or you can treat your sister with the respect she deserves."

Bot grimaces at the words. Mark frowns, glancing at the exit. The night grows quiet.

"You aren't a coward, Mark. If you were, you would have ended it instead of coming out here alone." Bot draws his gaze for a moment before it flicks back to the door. "She loves you and she's tougher than you think."

Mark raises a brow at the words.

"We can help, if you want it," Wolf offers again.

Mark's head shakes, almost involuntarily. "I've done all the programs, and they don't help."

"We aren't a program, brother. We are a family," Colin murmurs, looking at Wolf, who nods. "You don't need to decide this minute but just know we've got you tonight. We will get you through this."

Footsteps alert the three of them to the arrival of the others. Standing, Wolf steps out, leaving Bot to stay with Mark.

"Don't hurt her. Don't be like me. Be a better man." Mark stares at Bot, emotions skating over his face.

Bot jerks his head once, unwilling to voice a promise he's not sure he can make.

"Mark!" Her voice cuts through the night as she stumbles in, her momentum carrying her straight into her brother's body.

His arms come up and wrap around her, and Bot slides out silently. His team is spaced out, forming a perimeter around the small clearing. Erik is standing a few feet away from him, and Bot points to the right. The man follows him, a worried look in his eyes, eyes that are darting around trying to make sense of the situation.

As soon as they are out of earshot, he whispers, "How long has he been out here?"

Bot shakes his head. "From the looks of the shelter... Months." He glances back at Wolf, whose head in bent close to Joe's. "He's not coming back, at least not right now."

Erik's lips purse and his eyes fall shut for a moment.

"I'm not going to lie -- it's bad. He's bad but maybe one day, he will be ready for help." Joe's eyes lock on his at his words and his eyebrow raises.

Bot flips him the bird, pissed that he fell into this perfect trap.

"Did you two come up with this together?" He growls at Erik.

"What the fuck are you talking about, Bot?" He glances around before looking back at the young man he's come to call friend. "I didn't do anything but try to help Ruby. I knew if anyone could find him, you could."

"Sorry, man. I just..." He stops when Ruby steps out, tears running down her face.

He and Erik both move to her and he tries not to feel any jealousy when she turns to the other man for comfort.

"He won't come home." Her sobs are breaking his heart.

"We knew it wasn't likely, Red. I had hoped maybe, but at least we know where he is." She nods against his chest, trying to get control of herself. "Let me go talk to him and at least convince him to stay here where we can find him." He motions for Bot to take her.

Stepping away from her, he shoves down the anger he has for his friend and remembers it could have been him in these woods.

His ghosts are standing around the clearing, glaring at him like they do every minute of every day. He doesn't miss the knowing look on Wolf's face or the one of sympathy on Joe's. He hates that they can see through him so easily. They just nod, offering support if he needs it as he walks through the images of those he's lost or killed.

So much blood on his hands. On all their hands.

CHAPTER SEVENTEEN

Six months later.

Ruby sits at the small coffee shop. Bot watches from across the street as a smile lights up her face. His head turns to look just as Mark looks at him and nods. They have met once a month since that night.

Mark still refuses to come home or take their offer but once a month, he will come see her for as long as he can stand it. She takes what she can get. As he walks toward her, she looks at the other man from whom she's taking what can be given. The man she loves, the one she knows loves her.

He hasn't said it but he shows her every night. Ember was right -- it is a hard love that is scary but it is also amazing. She blows him a kiss, and he grins, then she looks back at her brother.

He sits and they talk until he suddenly shakes his head. "I love you," she whispers as he bolts up and is gone, disappearing around the corner. She has learned not to chase him and so she sits and clings to what little control she has on her emotions.

A warm hand on her shoulder makes the tears fall. It is

the same every month. He comes and leaves. She cries, and Colin holds her together.

"I'll be alright in a minute."

"I know." He draws her up and hugs her tight.

"Thank you for doing this with me. For keeping me from falling apart." She wipes her tears on his shirt and smiles because he never says a word about her using him as a tissue.

"I love you. I will always keep you together and if you do fall, I will be here to catch you." His voice is barely a whisper, but his arms are like steel bands.

HARD LOVE. Is there any better?

EPILOGUE

IT'S BEEN ANOTHER SIX MONTHS. MARK STILL WON'T COME home, and Ruby has quit asking. She's beginning to understand why he stays away. Still breaks her heart, but she at least knows he's alive.

She and Bot are still loving hard, splitting time between London and Colorado. She has sleepless nights when the team is out on a job and more sleepless nights when he gets home.

Ember is becoming a very good friend, and so are Joe and Wolf. She really likes the quiet Frenchman.

Bot still has moments where he wants to run but he loves her, and that's enough.

Each day, the shadows in his eyes fade a little, and he holds her a little tighter.

They are all fighting to find the person running the trafficking ring.

COMING SOON

SINNER PROTECTED

Prologue

The fire crackles in the small fireplace, its light bouncing off the walls of the darkened room. Jacques shifts gently in the worn rocking chair, trying to find a comfortable position. The stitches pull tightly at his irritated flesh; the last job had almost ended very badly. The client had been saved but barely.

He had let someone get too close, he had been sloppy. Distracted.

Old skeletons are surfacing.

His eyes turn to the picture on the mantle. He can't see the image clearly but then, he doesn't need to. He can see every detail in his mind. Her dark, curling hair and beautiful green eyes, rosy pink lips curved into a big smile. He can smell her perfume just like he had that day.

They had spent the entire day doing all the things they normally were allowed. Eating ice cream, visiting the village, so many things just the two of them. Until he had found them. Papa. He had brought them home and sent Jacques to his room. The walls of their home, no matter how beautifully painted, did not block the sound of his fist hitting her or her quiet cries.

Jacques squeezes his eyes tight, trying to stop the next memories... But they come.

It had been evening, the setting sun turning the sky the color of flames. She had called him to her room. Father had gone long ago. She had hugged him tightly, whispered so many words of love.

Of despair.
    Of regret.
    Of hope.

Then she had led him out onto the balcony. He watched as she climbed onto the ledge and turned to face him.

"je t'aime ma chère, mon bébé. Etre en sécurité, être fort."

He saw a moment of true peace right as she let herself fall.

He had been six. That was the day Wolf was born.

AFTERWORD

There are at least 20 Veteran Suicides Every Day

And that's just the official number. We think the number is more likely 24-25 Veterans a day. That is over 9,000 former service members each year we are losing to Veteran suicides. And the rate of active-duty suicides has increased over the last five years.

For every suicidal Veteran out there, there are 5-10 Veterans who are at risk. These Vets may be suffering from PTSD or Traumatic Brain Injury. They may be unemployed or suffering from other problems. They are often dealing with multiple issues that put them at risk for becoming suicidal.

Please consider supporting a veteran suicide program such as:
https://www.mission22.com/
https://nvf.org/stop-veteran-suicides/
Or any of the many others you can find.

ALSO BY RAVEN GALE

Coming soon

Sinner Protected: Sinner Security Series 2

Stay tuned for Jacques story, learn all about the Wolf.

Made in the USA
Columbia, SC
04 August 2024

39603771R00059